GW00725970

Spinoff

A NEW COMEDY

by Jack Sharkey

SAMUEL FRENCH, INC.

25 WEST 45TH STREET NEW YORK 10036
7623 SUNSET BOULEVARD HOLLYWOOD 90046
LONDON *TORONTO*

Printed in U.S.A.

ISBN 0 573 61602 7

For

TOM POSTON

and

FRANCESCA

CAST OF CHARACTERS

PETER COLTON, a minor bank official

LAUREL COLTON, his daughter

WILLY NICHOLAS, Peter's friend and—at the bank—superior

VICTORIA WICKEY, Peter's secretary

SHEILA MAHONEY, a travel agent

CARLOS ORTEGA, a delivery boy

TIME: *the present*

LOCALE: *the* COLTON *home in South Pasadena*

ACT ONE

An early Saturday afternoon in mid-March

ACT TWO

That evening

ACT THREE

Later that night

SPINOFF

ACT ONE

Curtain rises on the COLTON *home in South Pasadena. Most of what we see is the living room. A door in the lower Left wall leads off to* LAUREL COLTON'S *bedroom. Just above it in the same wall—but about eight inches higher than stage level—is the double-accordion door to a coat closet. On this same level, but in a wall at right angles to the first segment, is the front door to the house. When it is open, we will see a fraction of the front porch beyond it, the porch rail, and a large bush of semi-tropical aspect beyond the rail; beyond all the exterior sights is a southern California suburban backdrop—mostly sky, some trees, maybe a house or two in bright adobe-Spanish-stucco-modern architectural mismating. An adjoining L-shaped segment of wall—angling up right then suddenly down Right—houses a sofa, telephone table in the corner, and a large wing-back chair, all facing a low and uncluttered coffee-table. Right beside the wingback chair is an arch-way to a hallway which angles down Right toward the kitchen and rear of the house. On the continuation of the wall below the archway we find a broad functional desk, with a reasonably well-matching swivel chair before it. A small plain attache-case stands on the floor flush against the Downstage side of the desk, generally out of sight of anyone onstage. Just below the desk, in the same wall, is the door leading to* PETER COLTON'S *bedroom. The overall effect is one of brightness, cheer, and a woman's touch of neatness. It is a sunny early Saturday afternoon in mid-March.*

At curtain-rise, LAUREL COLTON *is Center stage, vacuuming; she is in her late teens, quite attractive, and energetic at her labors; her pretty housedress will not, however, get her on the Ten Best Dressed list, and her lovely hair is more-or-less bound back and hidden beneath a more functional than decorative bandanna. Over the sound of the vacuum cleaner, we hear the front door CHIMES sound. She hears them, turns off the vacuum cleaner, and starts for the door. Just before she gets there, CHIMES sound again.*

LAUREL. I'm *coming,* I'm *coming!* (*She opens door to reveal* WILLY NICHOLAS; *he is fortyish, well-dressed, and a bit distraught, but carrying himself well.*)

WILLY. (*Stepping into foyer.*) Laurel! I've got to talk to your father!

LAUREL. Dad's not home yet, Mister Nicholas.

WILLY. He's *got* to be! He left the bank before *I* did!

LAUREL. Did you come on foot?

WILLY. I sure did. I ran all the way!

LAUREL. That explains it. Dad's driving. In California, that takes a little longer. (*Behind* WILLY, *we see* CARLOS ORTEGA, *carrying a large bag of groceries, come up on the porch and toward front door; when we see* CARLOS *without the intervening bag, he will be a very handsome Spanish lad in his early twenties, dressed in a goodlooking slack/sportjacket combination and well-shined shoes.*)

WILLY. I must have passed him. I'll backtrack. (*Starts backing toward door.*)

LAUREL. Why don't you just wait for him? (*To* CARLOS, *who is just stepping into foyer:*) Hi, Carlos. Could you put that out in the kitchen?

CARLOS. Sure. (*Starts toward archway.*) Hi, Mister Nicholas.

WILLY. (*Distracted.*) Hi—uh-Carlos— (*To* LAUREL, *as* CARLOS *exits through archway.*) I *can't* wait for your father, I've got to see him right away! (*Starts out.*)

LAUREL. Mister Nicholas—is there anything wrong?

WILLY. (*Whirls back to face her.*) Wrong? What could be wrong? Nothing's wrong! (*Flashes sickly smile.*) Excuse me— (*Exits, shutting door;* LAUREL *takes step toward it, as if about to open it and continue her interrogation, then she gives it up and steps down into living room area just as* CARLOS *re-enters from kitchen through archway.*)

CARLOS. I put the milk and butter in the refrigerator.

LAUREL. Oh, thanks, Carlos . . . Say, aren't you kind of dressed up for delivering groceries?

CARLOS. Big date tonight. This way I don't have to go home and change.

LAUREL. Carlos, it's not even one o'clock. Won't you be all wrinkled and grubby by quitting time?

CARLOS. Not if I take it easy. And I always take it easy.

LAUREL. Even so, Carlos— Oh, how much do I owe you for the groceries?

CARLOS. Seventeen dollars and eighty-six cents.

LAUREL. For that one little order?

CARLOS. Well, if you're gonna buy all those fancy gourmet items like meat and bread—!

LAUREL. (*Starts for closet.*) Honestly, I don't know what prices are coming to! Last week I got almost the very same order for fifteen dollars . . . (*Will get purse from closet, money from purse, replace purse, close closet doors and come to him with money, during:*)

CARLOS. You're lucky *I* was filling your order. I grabbed the stuff from the back of the shelf where the *old* prices were still in effect.

LAUREL. You know, if my father's salary went up as fast as prices, we'd be millionaires.

CARLOS. Say, where *is* your father? I didn't know the bank was open Saturdays?

LAUREL. It's a new experiment they started this

month. Some of the customers complained about the six o'clock Friday closing, so the bank's seeing if Saturday morning hours make them any happier . . . (*Will give him the exact amount of money on:*) Nobody asked how *I* felt about it. Here. Frankly, I liked the old hours much better.

CARLOS. Look on the positive side: You can't clean on schooldays, and it's not easy with your father around, so the new banking hours give you a perfect chance to get all the housework done.

LAUREL. That's why I liked the old hours much better.

CARLOS. (*Laughs, pocketing the money.*) Don't put yourself down. You keep a great home for your dad.

LAUREL. I have to. With food prices so high, we sure can't afford a maid!

CARLOS. Didn't your father just get a promotion? That should bring in more dough.

LAUREL. Yes, but you'd hardly know it after deductions. And the jump from chief teller to operation manager isn't big enough to impress a flea!

CARLOS. That sounds like more money . . .

LAUREL. But it costs more to keep up appearances, now that he works outside the cage. For instance, he has to wear pants.

CARLOS. (*Laughs; then:*) Does the operation manager have the combination to the vault?

LAUREL. (*Rolls her eyes in chagrin.*) Don't even *tease* about that! It's all I think about, lately—all that money in the bank—and so little of it belongs to *us* . . . !

CARLOS. (*Starts for front door.*) Well, if he ever does get the combination, let me know. My uncle Luis used to be a passport forger . . . till he put two *n*'s in "Granada."

LAUREL. Believe it or not, I'll think it over! (*Both laugh at her jest; then, before he can open door:*) Oh, Carlos—what's that on the front of your pants?

CARLOS. (*Looks, grimaces.*) Oh, damn! The ice cream must have dripped! Do you have a—?

LAUREL. (*Jumps his line with:*) Get a wet cloth to it, quick! (*Is gesturing toward archway, although he is already headed that way; then she belatedly reacts.*) Oh! Did you put the *ice cream* in the refrigerator?

CARLOS. (*Hesitates at archway; then:*) Damn it, no, I forgot. I'll—

LAUREL. (*Hurrying his way.*) No, you take care of your pants, I'll see to the ice cream. (*She exits after him through archway; an instant later, the PHONE rings; we hear* LAUREL, *off.*) Talk about rotten timing—! Carlos, could you—?

CARLOS. (*Off. As* LAUREL *re-enters to grab up phone.*) I'll get the wet cloth *and* the ice cream!

LAUREL. (*On phone.*) Hello? . . . Oh, hello, Miss Wickey . . . No, Dad's not home yet . . . Yes, I expect him any minute . . . Sure, we're not going any place . . . Okay. 'Bye. (*Hangs up phone, sees vacuum cleaner in middle of room, goes to it and turns it on, starts vacuming again; as her back is turned to front door, CHIMES sound; she sighs in exasperation, turns off vacuum cleaner, and answers door.* PETER COLTON *stands there, with an attache case identical to the one beside the desk. He is well dressed in a dark suit, in about his mid-forties, and quite pleasant of aspect.*)

PETER. (*Steps into foyer, pecks her on cheek.*) Hi, honey.

LAUREL. Dad, have *you* misplaced your key *again?!*

PETER. (*Moving into living room, loosening necktie, setting attache case onto coffeetable.*) No, I just can't remember where I left it.

LAUREL. (*Shutting front door, coming in after him.*) Daddy, if a burglar finds one of those keys you keep losing, and gets into our house some day when we're out—

PETER. (*Slipping out of suit jacket, moving toward

bedroom.) He's in for a big disappointment! (*Pauses at bedroom door for.*) Unless you managed to ransom the television set? That'd be worth stealing.

LAUREL. Nope, still in the shop. (*With facetious nostalgia, as he exits into bedroom.*) How old was I when the man took it away?

PETER. (*Off.*) Who can remember that far back? . . . I wonder if that detective ever caught up with "The Fugitive"?

LAUREL. (*Moving to vacuum cleaner.*) That reminds me—Willy Nicholas was just here looking for you. (*Will stash vacuum against Upstage end of desk, during.*)

PETER. (*Off.*) What'd *he* want?

LAUREL. He didn't say. But it must be important. He seemed excited.

PETER. (*Off.*) Willy *always* seems excited. (*Will re-enter, tieless, in old comfortable-looking sleeveless pullover, during:*) He has a hyperactive thyroid and he drinks too much coffee.

LAUREL. He's probably bursting with some new joke he can't tell in front of me. Otherwise, he could have left a message.

PETER. Well, if he is, I'll tell it to you later.

LAUREL. That's what you *always* say!

PETER. (*Patting pockets vaguely.*) Now, what did I do with my cigarettes . . . ?

LAUREL. (*Helpfully, steps toward case on coffee-table.*) Maybe you stuck them in your case—

PETER. (*Almost violently lurches to case and grabs it up by both sides rather than by handle, defensively, on:*) *No!* I'm sure they're not in there! My jacket! They're in my jacket! I remember distinctly putting them in the pocket!

LAUREL. Daddy, you're *babbling* . . . You always babble when you're nervous . . .

PETER. Nervous? Me? Don't be silly! What would I be nervous about?

LAUREL. You're babbling again.

PETER. (*Still holding case by sides, hugs it against chest.*) Well—the way you keep accusing me of being nervous is enough to make anybody nervous!

LAUREL. Why are you clutching your case that way!

PETER. Case? What case? Oh, *this!* (*Gives forced laugh, and too matter-of-factly hefts case by handle and sets it on floor flush against lower end of sofa.*) Forgot I had it, that's all.

LAUREL. Now, Daddy, you're not going to leave it *there!* I've been trying to *clean* this place—

PETER. I'll move it, I'll move it! Uh, any other messages for me . . . ?

LAUREL. No, I don't think— Oh, yes, your secretary called.

PETER. Miss Wickey? Did she—uh—say what she wanted—?

LAUREL. (*Puzzled by his hesitancy, but not letting it show in her voice.*) No, she didn't. She said you'd know what it was.

PETER. Oh. Oh, yeah. I remember, now. It's business. That's all.

LAUREL. That's all I *thought* it was—till you said so.

PETER. What *else* could it be?

LAUREL. I'm not sure. Is she pretty?

PETER. Oh, come on, now. I thought *you* and *I* were an unbeatable team . . .

LAUREL. Never mind the gooey sentiment. Answer the question. Oh, wait, you won't have to. I can judge for myself when she stops by.

PETER. *Here?!*

LAUREL. Where else? . . . Daddy—is anything wrong?

PETER. Wrong? What could possibly be wrong? Nothing's wrong! (*Takes bottle of scotch out of lower drawer of Upstage end of desk, sets bottle on desk, shuts drawer, during.*) I'm just tired. Hard day. Not used to working Saturdays. That's all. So with your permission, I'm going to have a drink.

LAUREL. But, Dad—you almost *never* have a drink . . . ?!

PETER. No *wonder* I want one! (*Leaves bottle and starts for archway just as* CARLOS *enters from kitchen, looking spruced up and neat.*)

CARLOS. Hi, Mister Colton!

PETER. (*Stops beside him, looks from him to* LAUREL *and back; then:*) Is there something you two aren't telling me?

LAUREL. Carlos had a problem with his pants.

PETER. (*As though this is reassuring.*) Oh, is *that* all! (*Exits through archway toward kitchen.*)

LAUREL. Now I *know* something's bothering him!

CARLOS. (*Moving toward front door.*) Yes, he did take that rather well . . .

LAUREL. (*Sees attache case, picks it up and starts toward closet, on.*) Boy, is this thing heavy!

CARLOS. (*With mock hauteur.*) Don't call me "Boy"!

LAUREL. (*Still gamely lugging case across room.*) Oh, come off it, Carlos. I haven't picked on your nationality in weeks.

CARLOS. (*Coming forward to help her with case.*) I know. And oddly enough, I kind of miss it . . .

LAUREL. Well, you said you didn't like ethnic jokes—

CARLOS. I didn't mean you had to stop talking to me *entirely!*

LAUREL. (*They pause near lower corner of platform.*) Look, if you like my conversation, you'll like my jokes.

CARLOS. (*Resigned.*) Okay, I recognize the signs. What's the latest?

LAUREL. (*Eager to get a laugh out of him.*) Well, you've heard of the double-title movies—? Like "The High and the Mighty" and "The Agony and the Ecstasy" and "The Bad and the Beautiful"? Well, now they've made one about the Mexican who built the Golden Gate Bridge! . . .

CARLOS. (*Expects the worst, but asks gamely.*) What do they call it?

LAUREL. *"The Spick and the Span!"* (*She pauses hopefully; then* CARLOS *breaks down and snorts into laughter, which she joins.*) Isn't that terrible?

CARLOS. A definite ethnic insult. Wait'll I tell my uncle Luis!

LAUREL. That I insulted you?

CARLOS. No, the *joke,* stupid! (*As* LAUREL *laughs, he adds more seriously.*) I wish I didn't have that date tonight.

LAUREL. Me, too.

CARLOS. Hey? You wanta late-date? I can get Rosita home by nine o'clock!

LAUREL. Oh, I couldn't do that to another girl . . .

CARLOS. Do what? Her father wants her home by seven-thirty!

(*As* LAUREL *laughs at this, and both start toward closet again, the case somehow gets pulled open between them and tilts about one-hundred-seventy-six-thousand dollars onto the floor—most of it is bound into packets by paper cash straps, but a few loose bills scatter.* LAUREL *and* CARLOS *react and gasp in unison. Then:*)

LAUREL. Carlos! Look at all that money!

CARLOS. I'm *looking,* I'm *looking!* What kind of raise did your father *get,* anyway?! (*By reflex, both drop to knees and start cramming strap-packeted money back into case, though they will miss a few scattered single bills, on:*)

LAUREL. I knew this would happen! I just knew it! Prices going up and up and up—!

CARLOS. What are you worried about prices? This is a fortune!

LAUREL. But, Carlos, don't you know what this *means—?!*

CARLOS. Now, don't get excited, it might just be *business. . . .*

LAUREL. *Business?!*

CARLOS. Sure, maybe your father just brought it home to *count* it, or something—

LAUREL. (*Lurches to closet toting case in both arms, as* CARLOS *scurries about grabbing up loose bills.*) Don't you know *anything* about banks? Nobody gets out the *door* till every last transaction balances out to the *penny!* (*Heaves case into closet,* CARLOS *tosses loose bills in after it, both shut doors and lean back against them in agitated relief, during:*)

CARLOS. Now, look, Laurel—I'm sure there's a simple explanation—

LAUREL. (*Upset enough to clutch at straws, clutches his arm.*) Oh, Carlos, do you really think so?

CARLOS. Sure!

LAUREL. Such as? . . .

CARLOS. (*Thinks a second, then says lamely:*) He robbed the *bank!?*

LAUREL. Oh, Carlos! What are we going to do?!

CARLOS. (*Reacts, shies away, takes back-step toward front door.*) *"We"?* I mean . . . he's mostly *your* father . . . !

LAUREL. (*Clutching his hands.*) Oh, Carlos, please say you'll help me! *Por favor?*

CARLOS. Will you cut that out! You know I never speak Spanish! (*But he's weakening before her pleading gaze.*) Look . . . Laurel . . . I tell you what . . . I've gotta get back to work, now, but later, maybe, I can come back, and—

LAUREL. (*As, unseen by her,* PETER *re-enters with tumbler of ice cubes and goes to desk where he will pour drink.*) I don't know if I can *wait* till nine o'clock—!

PETER. (*Engrossed in pouring.*) Why, what happens at nine o'clock?

LAUREL. (*She and* CARLOS *both jump in shock.*) Dad! When did *you* get back—?!

PETER. (*With mild puzzlement.*) I haven't been *away . . . ?*

CARLOS. (*Anxious to get out of this, back toward door.*) Well, look, you and your father probably have lots to talk about, so I'll just be getting back to work, and— (*Has managed to open door behind him and slip out.*) See you later! (*Shuts door after him.*)

PETER. (*Idly curious, crosses toward her, carrying drink.*) What did he mean, "talk about"? Do we have something to talk about?

LAUREL. (*Faces him, forlorn in her despair.*) Oh, Daddy . . . ! It's too *late* to talk *now!* (*With a wail of unhappiness, flees into her bedroom, shutting door after her.*)

PETER. (*Bewildered, starts toward bedroom door.*) Laurel—? Honey, what's wrong?

LAUREL. (*Off. With unhappy mockery.*) Wrong? Nothing's *wrong!* What could possibly be wrong? (*Door CHIMES sound before* PETER *can quite open bedroom door to go in after her.*) You'd better get the door, Daddy.

PETER. But honey—

LAUREL. (*Off.*) It's all right. I just want to lie down for awhile—and think— (*Door CHIMES sound again; reluctantly,* PETER *abandons his position and opens front door;* WILLY *lurches in, slams door behind him, leans against it.*)

WILLY. I *drove* back here this time. That's what took so long.

PETER. Laurel *said* you were looking for me— (*Stops as* WILLY *abruptly removes glass from his hand, drains it, and hands it back empty.*)

WILLY. (*Miserably.*) Thanks.

PETER. (*Mustering his etiquette.*) Don't mention it. Would you—like another?

WILLY. (*Running fingers through hair at the temples, lurches into the room, dazed, a practically broken man.*) It doesn't help. Nothing helps. I'm losing my mind. (*Sinks onto sofa, burying face in hands for:*) It's so awful—I don't know what to do—where to turn— (*raises face to say, savoring after-taste:*) Maybe I will have another, just a small one. No. A big one. (*As a puzzled-but-polite* PETER *goes to bottle with glass.*) How long does it take to get cirrhosis—?

PETER. (*Will pour drink, bring it to him, etc, during:*) Oh, hours and hours. Now you just calm down a little, and— Here you go, buddy—you and I can—

WILLY. (*Punctuating between phrases with sips of drink.*) I can't! . . . I wish I could! . . . I wish I was dead! . . . Oh, Pete—!

PETER. Now, now, nothing's as bad as all that . . . (*Sits in wingback chair, then asks amicably.*) Suppose you just relax and tell me what's the matter.

WILLY. (*Hesitates, takes sip of drink for courage, then stares off in front of him with faraway look, on:*) I robbed the bank today. (*After a pregnant pause, looks at* PETER.) Well? Aren't you going to *say* anything?

PETER. (*To help it sink in, slowly repeats:*) You robbed the bank today.

WILLY. I *know* that! (*Takes gulp of drink.*) Well?

PETER. Well what? What am I supposed to say, *congratulations?!*

WILLY. Of *course* not! You're supposed to say you'll *help* me!

PETER. How? You need a lift to the airport?

WILLY. *Air*port?!

PETER. I'm kind of a novice at these things, but—don't all bank robbers catch the next flight to Rio?

WILLY. Rio? That costs a fortune!

PETER. What did you rob, anyhow—desk blotters?!

WILLY. Oh. You mean the money. I couldn't spend *that,* Pete, it doesn't *belong* to me!

PETER. What *are* you planning to do with it—fondle it?

WILLY. Fondle it? Pete, I don't even *have* it! (*Takes large unhappy swallow of drink.*)

PETER. Did I walk into the *middle* of this conversation, or *what?* Let's take it from the top— You robbed the bank today— (WILLY *nods miserably.*) And you took real money, not desk blotters— (WILLY *nods even more miserably, lower lip trembling.*) But you have no plans for the money because you haven't got it?

WILLY. Of course I have plans for it! I was going to take it to Mister Pelsner!

PETER. The president of the bank? Our boss?

WILLY. There's *another* Mister Pelsner?

PETER. But Willy—why? Why would you rob the bank and then take the money to the bank president?

WILLY. I was hoping to get a promotion.

PETER. For robbing the bank?!

WILLY. No, for taking the money out of the vault!

PETER. Aren't you sort of—splitting hairs?

WILLY. Pete, you don't understand—I didn't *mean* to rob the bank . . .

PETER. It was an *accident?!*

WILLY. (*Exasperated, forgets to be unhappy, sets down tumbler on coffeetable and says, with irate control:*) Listen! Do you remember Monday morning's staff meeting?

PETER. I usually try to *forget* staff meetings.

WILLY. But you remember attending—?

PETER. I must have. I haven't been fired.

WILLY. Look, let me jog your memory—old man Pelsner was boasting about the bank's security system.

PETER. He's always boasting about it. It's his pride and joy.

WILLY. Right. And that's what inspired me to rob the bank.

PETER. You wanted to break his heart.

WILLY. *No!* I wanted to show him there's a *flaw* in the *security* system!

PETER. You know—you're almost beginning to make sense . . . Wait a minute! What flaw? Every penny is counted before the vault is locked. Nobody gets out until they total every check and check every total—

WILLY. Sure. But once the vault is locked what do they do . . . ?

PETER. They relax and let everybody go home. They *have* to let us go, *sometime!*

WILLY. But Pete, don't you see the flaw?

PETER. Not with a time-lock on the vault, no. Nobody can open the door again till an hour before the next bank opening.

WILLY. But who sets the time-lock . . . ?

PETER. Willy!

WILLY. Right!

PETER. Now, hold on—you need two combinations —and no vice president knows more than one—

WILLY. Pete, bank officers are notoriously lazy.

PETER. Speak for yourself. I'm just Operation Manager.

WILLY. Look, they got bored spinning the dial after the vault is shut. I started doing it for them. They just sign the book that the vault has been locked. It saves them the bother of coming down by the vault every day at quitting time. (*As the plan dawns on* PETER, *he begins talking faster, as does* WILLY, *and the next fourteen lines are spoken quite rapidly, the conversational ball going from one man to the other as in a tennis tournament, each edging a bit forward on his speech, then starting to rise, till both are standing at end.*)

PETER. Willy—! I think I'm beginning to *get* it—! *Today* you set the time-lock *early*—

WILLY. For a half-hour after closing—

PETER. You waited till the guard shut the vault—

WILLY. I spun the one dial whose combination I knew—

PETER. Only *pretended* to spin the other one—!

WILLY. So when the guard tried the handle—!

PETER. The vault was locked!

WILLY. And then in half an hour—

PETER. You dialed *your* combination—

WILLY. Opened the vault and put one-hundred-seventy-six-thousand dollars in small bills into my attache case and took it out!

PETER. As simple as that!

WILLY. So I could show old man Pelsner the flaw in the system—

PETER. A flaw named Willy Nicholas!

WILLY. Don't I know it! (*Both are standing, now;* WILLY *starts for desk on:*) I need another drink.

PETER. (*Starts for kitchen on:*) I think I'll get a glass and join you . . . (*Exits, but continues, off:*) I think I see what you were up to, but—wasn't actually *robbing* the bank a little *drastic—?!*

WILLY. (*Refilling his glass.*) You mean, why didn't I simply *tell* him?

PETER. (*Off.*) Yeah!

WILLY. (*With glass in hand, filled, says dreamily, out front.*) Sure, sure. I can hear myself now: (*In adolescent boyish singsong:*) "Hey, guess *what,* Mister Pelsner! I'm the *only* one of your *trusted* employes who *knows* how to *rob* your *bank!*" (*Shudders, takes a sip, then as* PETER *re-enters with another tumbler of ice, to him:*) He would have put *handcuffs* on me!

PETER. (*Filling own glass.*) Or a straitjacket. Yeah, I understand now. Telling him might have cost you your job, but giving him the stolen money would prove your honesty!

WILLY. (*Suspecting sarcasm.*) Well, it *would!*

PETER. I know, I know! Crazy as it sounds, it makes sense. But wait a minute—you say you haven't *got* the money? Why not? Your scheme didn't work, or what?

WILLY. Oh, it worked. I got the money just fine. Then I lost it.

PETER. (*Almost chokes on drink.*) *Lost* it?! One-hundred-seventy-six-thousand dollars—?!

WILLY. (*Miserably.*) In small bills.

PETER. (*Leading way over to sofa, where they will both sit, side by side,* PETER *at the Upstage end.*) But Willy—how *could* you lose that money—?

WILLY. I don't know. That's the horrible part. I've gone over and over the whole thing in my head, retraced my moves step by step—

PETER. (*Places calming hand on* WILLY's *shoulder.*) Now, listen, you've *got* to remember! What exactly did you do from the time you put the money in your case?

WILLY. (*Racking his brain.*) Well . . . I—I shut the vault . . .

PETER. Where was the case?

WILLY. In my right hand. I shut the door with my left hand. Then I put the case in my other hand.

PETER. Okay-okay. Then what?

WILLY. (*Shuts his eyes to help his concentration.*) Then . . . I . . . took the money up to . . . the main floor area . . .

PETER. Fine, you're doing fine, keep going . . .

WILLY. (*Opens eyes.*) That's *it! Now* I remember! I hadn't tried the handle on the vault door to be sure it was *locked*—

PETER. What did it matter? You cleaned the place *out—?!*

WILLY. Who knows? Neatness! Force of habit! Temporary insanity!

PETER. Okay-okay. So you went back and locked it—

WILLY. Not quite.

PETER. You didn't go *back* or you didn't check the *handle?*

WILLY. Both. You see, Pete—I remembered that, after I showed the money to Pelsner, I'd have to put it all back. I mean, I couldn't keep it till Monday in my *apartment!*

PETER. Oh, yeah. Never thought of that. Okay, go on.

WILLY. So I stood there on the stairs, thinking . . .

PETER. About what?

WILLY. Old man Pelsner. I mean—*you* know how he is—no sense of humor or anything—?

PETER. Do I ever! But what's that got to do with—?

WILLY. All at once I thought: "What if he doesn't see it my way? What if he just sees the money and starts screaming *'Thief! Thief!'* "

PETER. Now *there's* a horrible image!

WILLY. Right! So I started thinking—

PETER. A bit belatedly—

WILLY. (*Ignores this jab, and goes on:*) Maybe it *wasn't* such a smart idea after all. Maybe it was the dumbest thing I'd ever done in my life! Here I was, a trusted employe, with all the bank's assets in my attache case. The more I thought, the scareder I got. I mean, look at the thing objectively: I'd set the time-lock wrong—I'd lied about spinning the other dial—I'd looted the vault— (*Turns to* PETER *and says solemnly:*) It seemed like a pretty flimsy way to demonstrate my honesty.

PETER. It's not exactly shatterproof.

WILLY. So I hurried back upstairs to where I'd left the attache case—

PETER. (*Comes to his feet on:*) *Left* the *attache case—?!*

WILLY. Well, I was nervous.

PETER. (*Making half-gestures, all ineffectual, partly pacing.*) *Left* the *attache case—!*

WILLY. I put it down next to the drinking fountain before I started back toward the vault.

PETER. A hundred-seventy-six-thousand dollars? *In small bills—?!*

WILLY. I *had* to leave it. I sure as hell didn't want to be caught *carrying* it!

PETER. But—! But—! But—! Oh, hell, go on with your story.

WILLY. Well, when I got back upstairs to the drinking fountain—

PETER. Which one?

WILLY. The one near the general offices. You ought to know—when you were chief teller you must have gone there six times a day!

PETER. My tongue got yucky licking all those cash straps.

WILLY. What about your sponge dish?

PETER. I kept forgetting to put water in it.

WILLY. Can't you remember anything? You let your dish go dry, you keep misplacing door keys, and the other day you even forgot your own telephone number!

PETER. I've had things on my mind. You see, I've been planning a sort of surprise for Laurel—

WILLY. Even so, Pete, sometimes I think you're not very bright!

PETER. (*Throws up his hands in exasperation.*) *You* lose a hundred-seventy-six-thousand dollars, and *I'm* not very bright? (*Sits, shaking head, as* WILLY *belatedly reacts.*)

WILLY. Good grief, I almost *forgot* about that! (*Clutches* PETER's *hand.*) Pete, you've got to help me!

PETER. *How?!*

WILLY. Please don't say no!

PETER. I didn't say no, I said how!

WILLY. Then you'd help me if you could?

PETER. Of course I would!

WILLY. (*Drops* PETER's *hand, leans back with happy sigh.*) Good, that makes you an accessory after the fact.

PETER. What?!

WILLY. Now you can't turn me in.

PETER. (*Smacks palm to forehead, stands on:*) Willy, this is crazy! I'm trying to help you, and you're—

WILLY. (*Slides forward almost onto his knees from sofa, clutching both* PETER's *hands.*) I'm crazed with fear, I'll say anything! . . . *Please* help me!

PETER. Well—we could check out every employe who was in the bank when the money vanished . . .

WILLY. You think an employe got it?

PETER. It has to be an employe. The bank was already locked for the day.

WILLY. (*Rises to face* PETER, *a spark of hope in his eye.*) You're right! It's got to be an inside job.

PETER. So all we've got to do is find him—

WILLY. (*Clutches* PETER'S *shoulder.*) Wait! When we find him—what do we say? "You ran off with the money I stole!"?

PETER. Look, we'll think of something when that time comes. Right now, we've got to find the money, quick, before whoever took it looks in your case and phones the police!

WILLY. Then you don't think they took it on purpose?

PETER. We can't be sure, of course—most likely it was a mistake . . .

WILLY. But what if it *was* on purpose?! What if whoever took it is on his way to Rio already?!

PETER. Then the police will go after *him,* and *you're* in the *clear!*

WILLY. Hey—that's beautiful! (*Suddenly conspiratorial.*) Listen, Pete—why don't we just *phone* everybody, one at a time, and *tell* whoever it is that there's a plane leaving for Rio, and—

PETER. Willy, you wouldn't tempt anyone like that? You wouldn't make such terrible trouble for an innocent man?

WILLY. Why not? *I'm* in terrible trouble, and *I'm* an innocent man?! (*Wilts before* PETER'S *scornful gaze.*) Okay-okay, so we'll go find them— Hey, do you know the addresses of the other employes?

PETER. There are less than a dozen—they must be in the phone book—

WILLY. You're right. Okay, what are their names?

PETER. Search *me!*

WILLY. Come on, you *must* know them. Think. We can start with—uh—that tall guy—Bill um—what's-his-name . . . Pete—what's Bill's last name?

PETER. Bill who?

WILLY. (*Goes to reply, realizes he can't; sags.*) Oh, boy, this is worse than I thought! (*Suddenly snaps fingers.*) Wait a minute! Your secretary, Miss Wickey —*she* must know the name of every man in the bank!

PETER. What makes you think so?

WILLY. I've seen Miss Wickey! She's the kind of girl if she didn't ask a guy for his name, he'd *volunteer* the information—*and* his phone number!

PETER. Yes, but can we ask for her help without telling her what she's helping *with?* The fewer people know what you did, the better.

WILLY. We'll tell her just enough of the truth.

PETER. How much is just enough?

WILLY. We say my case was full of important papers. We don't have to say the government printed them!

(PETER *nods and starts dialing phone; as he does,* LAUREL *emerges from her bedroom. The bandanna is gone from her hair and she has changed to a pretty dress and freshened her face a bit. Her face is calm, but set with determination. She carries a small clutch-purse. Seeing no one—the two men are Upstage in their area near the phone— she goes to the closet, opens the door stoops and retrieves several of the loose bills, which she stuffs into her purse, then carefully shuts the closet again, and starts to ever-so-gently let herself out the front door. During this, however:*)

PETER. (*On phone.*) Hello? . . . Oh, hi, Muriel, is your roommate there? . . . This is Mister Colton . . . Oh, of course! I'd forgotten! Thank you! . . . (*Hangs up, says to* WILLY.) She's on her way over here right now.

WILLY. Muriel? What for? (*At this point,* LAUREL *has door open, and* VICTORIA WICKEY, *carrying long envelope, steps up on porch behind her; she is definitely the type to whom men volunteer their phone numbers, about twenty-six years old with measurements slightly larger than her I.Q.;* LAUREL *bumps into her and jumps, then sees who it is, puts a finger to her lips, and lets the newcomer in, then quietly lets herself out and quietly shuts the door after her. All this during the continuation of the* PETER/WILLY *conversation:*)

PETER. Not Muriel, Miss Wickey!

(*Over next six lines,* VICKI *will stand hesitantly, giving a bewildered belated wave after the departed* LAUREL, *then look around blankly, hear voices, and timidly move toward them, arriving just behind* WILLY *before her line;* PETER, *of course, is looking a bit angrily toward Downstage Right, away from* WILLY, *so does not see her approach, either, till she speaks.*)

WILLY. Why's she coming *here?*

PETER. We have some business to discuss.

WILLY. What business? Remember, Pete, I'm your boss, an assistant vice president. I know the rules, and you have no business having a business discussion after business hours!

PETER. It's *personal* business!

WILLY. *What* personal business?

PETER. That's *my* business!

VICKI. I can come back later if you're talking business. (*Both men react, turn to her.*)

PETER. Miss Wickey!

WILLY. How did *you* get here?

VICKI. (*As though he'd asked, "How did you get here?"*) Bill gave me a lift on his Honda. (*Sets envelope on coffeetable.*)

WILLY. Hey, do you know what Bill's last name is—?!

VICKI. No, what?

PETER. (*As* WILLY *groans.*) Never mind that! Did Bill have a *case* with him?

VICKI. No, but I think he was on his way to buy a *fifth* . . .

WILLY. An *attache* case, like mine!

VICKI. Well, sure!

PETER. What do you mean, "sure!"?

VICKI. Mister Nicholas is an *officer*. So *everybody* bought a case like his.

WILLY. Damn it, she's right! I *do* get imitated by my underlings—

PETER. (*Surprised and resentful.*) *"Underlings"!?*

WILLY. (*Self-correcting with more impatience than politeness.*) Subordinates!

PETER. (*Distracted from resentment by sudden thought.*) Hey, listen—that may be it—I mean, so many cases, all looking alike—it almost *has* to mean the pickup was by mistake!

VICKI. No, I *asked* Bill for a lift.

WILLY. (*Nearly explosively.*) He's referring to a *different* kind of pickup!

VICKI. (*Missing the open innuendo, with bright acceptance.*) Oh.

PETER. Hey. How did you get *in* here, *anyhow*, Miss Wickey?

VICKI. Laurel let me in on her way out.

PETER. She went out? Did she say where she was going?

VICKI. She didn't say a word.

PETER. Then how did you know who she was?

VICKI. I recognized her face.

PETER. (*Almost to himself.*) Come to think of it, how did *she* know who *you* were . . . ? (*Recovers, speaks directly to* VICKI.) I'm sorry, it's something Laurel said earlier about you. Somehow, I got the impression you hadn't *met . . . ?*

WILLY. (*At the end of his rope.*) So *introduce* them, sometime! Talk over their family *trees!* But right *now* can we get back to *my* problem—?

VICKI. What problem, Mister Nicholas?

WILLY. None of your business!

VICKI. Then how can we get back to it?

PETER. (*To calm the growing storm.*) Listen, why

don't you two sit down and relax, while I get a glass for Miss Wickey? (*To* VICKI.) Do you *like* Scotch on the rocks?

WILLY. (*Almost an "aside."*) You'd better. It's all he's got.

VICKI. (*Brightly.*) I can *learn—!?*

PETER. (*Stepping toward archway.*) I'll be right back. (*Exits.*)

VICKI. (*Turns to* WILLY.) Mister Nicholas—

WILLY. Miss Wickey— (*Then, with stunning suddenness, they are in each others' arms, hugging, fondling, caressing, during:*) Vicki!

VICKI. Willy!

WILLY. Oh, my sweet darling!

VICKI. Sweetheart! Beloved! (*They kiss, recklessly, violently; then she breaks away for:*) Do you think he suspects?

WILLY. Not a thing. Do you have the airline tickets? (VICKI *hands him envelope.*)

VICKI. Nine o'clock, non-stop, California to Rio, fly-now-pay-later. Did you get the passports?

WILLY. (*Pats jacket inner-pocket.*) Right here. You saw him leave with the case? (*Puts envelope in same inner pocket.*)

VICKI. I handed it to him before he left his desk. Did he fall for the bit about the drinking fountain?

WILLY. I think so. I haven't suggested his part in it, yet. But he's so absent-minded he's sure to swallow it.

VICKI. You'd better finish. When he comes back, I'll go powder my nose, and you spin the *rest* of the web!

WILLY. Right! (*They kiss again, frantically, madly, then break for:*) I think he's coming!

VICKI. Hang in there, Willy! (*Both are smoothing clothing, unmussing hair, etc.*)

WILLY. Don't worry!

VICKI. Only a few more hours—!

WILLY. And then . . . !

VICKI. And *then* . . . ! (*Sensing* PETER'S *proximity, leaps into:*) . . . I said to him, "Say, what kind of girl do you think I *am?*" and *he* said, "That depends on your answer to the *question!*"

WILLY. (*As* PETER *enters with tumbler of ice, headed for desk.*) So what was your answer to the question?

VICKI. (*Who had been improvising out of whole cloth, blankly:*) *What* question?

PETER. (*Pouring Scotch over her rocks.*) Who are you talking about, Fatherless Bill?

WILLY. Fatherless Bill—?

PETER. Well, he doesn't seem to have a *surname—! (Comes with drink to* VICKI.) *There* you go, Miss Wickey!

VICKI. (*Takes sip, smiles.*) Mmm, that's good. (*Hands glass to* WILLY.) I have to go to the bathroom. (*Exits through archway.*)

WILLY. (*As* PETER *stares, fascinated, after her.*) Kidney trouble. (*As* PETER *reacts with uncertainty, changes subject.*) Pete—do you know what *this* is—? (*On stress-word, pulls key from pocket, holds it up.*) It's a key to your house.

PETER. (*Amiably curious.*) Where did you get the key to my house?

WILLY. Your *daughter* gave it to me! (*As* PETER *stares blankly.*) You're supposed to say "You swine!"

PETER. (*Amiably playing the game.*) You swine.

WILLY. Oh, come on, Pete, don't you wonder *why* Laurel gave me a key?

PETER. Well, yes, but not in the *you-swine* sense. I mean, I have nothing but confidence in my daughter. But—why *did* she give you a key?

WILLY. I thought you had confidence in her . . . ?

PETER. I do. It's *you* I'm *uncertain* about!

WILLY. You never distrusted me *before . . . ?!*

PETER. (*Shrugs, says logically:*) You never robbed the *bank* before!

WILLY. (*Rolls eyes heavenward with a groan;*

then:) She gave me the key because you keep losing yours, and she thought I should carry a spare for you in case you ever got locked out when she wasn't home, okay?!

PETER. What a thoughtful *kid—!*

WILLY. Now, let's get down to the reason behind this reasoning: *Where* is your attache case?

PETER. (*Glances about, vaguely.*) It was here a minute ago—maybe Laurel put it away . . . (*Then, puzzled.*) What's that got to do with you having a key to my house?

WILLY. (*Claps amiable hand on his shoulder.*) Pete—look at it from my point of view: You forget things. You do things automatically without being aware of them. Isn't it the most natural thing in the world that I wonder if—just perhaps—*you* might have picked up that case of mine—?

PETER. Oh. Yes, I see. Yeah, but look, Willy, I may forget to *do* things now and then—but I don't remember forgetting things I've already *done—!*

WILLY. See? You don't remember!

PETER. I mean I remember perfectly well what I've *done.* I just forget things I'm *supposed* to do.

WILLY. Like what?

PETER. (*Beat; then, embarrassed:*) Like what I forgot to remember I've done. (*Then with more spunk.*) But listen, you're being ridiculous. I'd surely remember taking a drink *without* a satchel, then leaving the drinking fountain *with* one!

WILLY. Pete—buddy, old friend—face it—*you* never remember *anything!* And you *always* stop for a drink at the fountain before you leave the bank. My case was sitting right there. You probably picked it up by *reflex . . . !*

PETER. I've never stolen anything in my life—so how could I do it by *reflex—?!*

WILLY. Listen, you told me in the drugstore—

PETER. What drugstore?

WILLY. When we went out for coffee today.

PETER. Was that today? I thought we went out Wednesday . . .

WILLY. See?! See what I mean?!

PETER. (*Uncomfortable, shifts the subject back a pace.*) Told you *what* in the drugstore?

WILLY. That you couldn't remember bringing your attache case to work this morning—

PETER. Say, as a mater of fact, I *don't* remember bringing it to work this morning!

WILLY. And yet—you brought it home this afternoon?

PETER. (*Stymied, trying to remember details.*) I—well—*yes!* . . . I mean—I brought *a* case home this afternoon . . . (*Stares roundabout him for the missing case, guiltily.*)

WILLY. You know what *I* think—?

PETER. (*Apprehensively.*) . . . What—?

(VICKI *enters, all smiles, through archway.*)

VICKI. Hi!

WILLY. (*Hands her her drink, gives unseen-by-* PETER *"scram" signal.*) Here!

VICKI. (*Gets message, takes sip, then widens eyes for:*) I have to go to the bathroom! (*Gallops out archway,* PETER *staring wide-eyed after her.*)

WILLY. That poor kid!

PETER. (*Shaking off amazement, back to* WILLY.) Never mind her kidneys! *What* do you think, Willy—?

WILLY. *I* think you probably picked up *my* case!

PETER. But—

WILLY. You don't remember bringing it to work this morning—?

PETER. Well . . . *no* . . . but— (*Brightens as possible explanation occurs to him.*) I probably left it at the bank last night! Easy thing to do. Then, today, I see it, pick it up, take it out with me . . . (*Stops because* WILLY *is sadly shaking his head.*)

WILLY. Pete . . . (PETE *stops extemporizing, looks at him solemnly.*) Can we just *look* at your case . . . ?

PETER. But I *know* what's in my case!

WILLY. If it *is* your case! (*Then, puzzled.*) *What's* in your case?

PETER. (*Beaten, stoical:*) I guess you may as well know— Travel brochures about Rio!

WILLY. *Rio?!* Where the *bank robbers* go—?!

PETER. It was Miss Wickey's idea.

WILLY. Robbing our bank?

PETER. No, Rio! I wanted a neat place to take Laurel on a surprise vacation next week, during the spring holiday from school. Miss Wickey thought Rio would be just the place.

WILLY. But why are you still carrying them around?

PETER. (*Exasperated.*) *Laurel* doesn't know about the vacation. It's a *surprise!* How could I leave all that Technicolor literature around *here?!*

WILLY. Okay-okay, that's what's in *your* case! But can't we just take a peek to make sure you didn't wander home with *mine?*

PETER. Oh, for heaven's *sake—!* (PETER *looks about, between sofa and wingback chair, under coffeetable, then looks sheepish, for:*) I guess Laurel put it away somewhere. She was cleaning today— (*Gestures mechanically at vacuum cleaner.*) I shouldn't have left it on the coffeetable . . .

WILLY. (*Just the tiniest bit apprehensive.*) And— Laurel just went *out*—and didn't say where she was going—?!

PETER. Oh, come off it, Willy! The case is around here someplace . . . (*Has been prowling about as he converses, now spots attache case beside desk, and brightens for:*) See? What did I tell you! There it is! (*Totes case back to coffeetable, just as* VICKI *makes a second re-entrance through archway, and* WILLY *leans in close to case as* PETER *starts to open it.*)

WILLY. C'mon, c'mon, open it!

PETER. (*Straightens from task, shrugs.*) I can't. It's locked.

VICKI. Where's the key?

PETER. With my house key.

WILLY. Hold it! It *can't* be locked if it's *my* attache case!

PETER. I *told* you I was pretty sure I didn't take your case . . .

VICKI. But you *did!* I know it for a fact! (PETER *stares at her, intrigued by her assurance, while behind him* WILLY *wigwags danger-signals to her, which—after a blank moment—she comprehends, and:*) I mean—if you *didn't*—who *did?*

WILLY. (*Realizes:*) Hey, I just thought—let's use *my* key on it! If it's my case, it should open right up!

VICKI. (*Brightly, as* WILLY *fumbles out a key ring.*) And if it isn't, it won't!

WILLY. Thank you, Albert Einstein! (*Has flipped to proper key, starts trying it in lock.*) Now, this should just pop open and—and— That's funny . . . ?!

PETER. (*Starting to pick up case.*) I *told* you it couldn't be yours— (WILLY *snatches case from him.*) Hey!

WILLY. *I* know what! I'll take it to my place. I'm sure I have a crowbar somewhere, and—

PETER. (*Snatches it back.*) Now *just* a *minute—!* That's my personal property!

WILLY. It's mine!

PETER. Then why doesn't your key work?

WILLY. *I* don't know! It's bent! The lock is rusty! The spring is jammed! Who cares?!

PETER. Now look, I know you've been under a strain, but this is a pretty expensive case, Willy! (*Sets it down carefully on coffeetable.*) If you'll just keep calm a few moments, I'll go look for a spare key in Laurel's room, and we can settle this whole thing! (*Starts toward* LAUREL's *bedroom door, during:*)

VICKI. How do you know she's got one?

PETER. Laurel's got spares of *all* my keys. If she

hasn't given them away to Willy! (*Exits into bedroom as* WILLY *reacts.*)

WILLY. (*Fumbling through keys on ring.*) Hey, I think she *did* give me one of his case keys . . . now where the—?

VICKI. But if you have it, and it opens, it'll *prove* it's his case—?!

WILLY. (*Still searching for key.*) How *can* it be? You *handed* him my case, *didn't* you—?! (*Finds key, starts fiddling in lock with it.*) I probably accidentally tried *his* key on the case, before. *That's* why it didn't open. So that means *this* key is *mine,* and—Ah! (*Triumphantly turns key in lock.*) There, you see?

VICKI. You're a genius. I always said so. Can I see the money?

WILLY. We should wait for Pete . . .

VICKI. Why? If he finds *another* key, he'll come out and *lock* it again!

WILLY. (*Indulgently.*) Oh, all right! (*Flips case open, and a cascade of colorful travel brochures—for Rio, Mexico and the Caribbean—pours onto the coffee-table;* WILLY's *eyes bug in horror.*) What the hell is all *this* junk?!

VICKI. (*More bemused than aghast.*) Why—those are the travel brochures I've been getting Mister Colton.

WILLY. (*Drained, dazed.*) *You've* been getting—?

VICKI. Yes, that's how I know Laurel. Men don't understand these things. You can't just take a young girl off on a surprise trip without her having a chance to buy anything wonderful to wear. So when he *told* me about the *surprise, I* told *her*—of course, I told her *she'd* have to keep the secret I was keeping from *her* from *him,* if you know what I mean, because I wouldn't want my boss to know I couldn't keep a secret *secret,* because he'd be upset and—*mmmmph!* (*This last sound is caused by a large hand over her mouth; the hand belongs to* WILLY; *he has been trying to stop this flood of drivel with half-gestures and frantic guppy-mouthing attempts at speech, and has all at once decided this is the only way. He stands there a second, dangerously quiet; she stands there, too, eyes bewildered and wide; after about two beats, convinced he has stemmed the flow, he removes his hand and speaks with low, husky, urgent intensity.*)

WILLY. Vicki . . . Where—is—my—*money!?*

VICKI. (*Thinks a moment—and, for her, it's not easy; then:*) Maybe Mister Colton found it and gave it back.

WILLY. (*Every minute going deeper into shock.*) Don't say that! He's got to have it! It's around here someplace, I'm sure of it! We've got to search . . . everywhere . . . right away . . . that plane's taking off at nine o'clock!

VICKI. But if we search, he'll think we don't *trust* him . . . ?!

WILLY. (*Suddenly galvanized, starts stuffing brochures back into the case, which he will quickly snap shut, during:*) Listen, there's no time to explain—when Pete comes back, I want you to listen carefully to everything I say, and play along, got me?! I'm going to have one of my spells . . .

VICKI. What spells?

WILLY. Damn it, will you play along?! I don't *have* spells, but I want Pete to think— Oh-oh, here he comes! Act nonchalant! (*Both go into a regular* risus sardonicus *of smiling innocence as* PETER *re-enters from bedroom, scratching his head in puzzlement; he sees them and stops.*)

PETER. What's wrong?

VICKI. (*In a voice tinkling with happy laughter:*) Wrong? Nothing's wrong! What could possibly be wrong?

PETER. (*Continues his interrupted trek toward them.*) You both looked so happy I thought your minds had snapped.

WILLY. Never mind our minds, where's the key?

PETER. I couldn't find one. I thought I knew where she kept them, but—

VICKI. (*Inspired.*) Maybe you boys didn't try hard enough . . . (*Bends over case, flicking latch open on:*) Sometimes these locks are just a little tricky— Ah! (*As before, the case opens and the brochures cascade.*)

WILLY. (*Goes overemphatically wild-eyed with simulated shock.*) *Aaaaaaah!* (*Clutches at wrong side [the right side] of chest, on:*) Oh! I think it's my heart! (*Lurches backward into sag onto sofa.*) I was afraid this would happen—all the strain—the fear—! (*Really hams up gasps, twinges and twitches.*)

VICKI. (*To* PETER, *in a misconceived conspiratorial "aside."*) It's one of his spells.

PETER. (*Had frozen, now springs toward* WILLY.) Good heavens, Willy—! I'll call a doctor—!

WILLY. (*Waving feeble hand, etc.*) N-no! No doctor! They have to make police reports! (*Fumbles in pocket.*) P-p-pills! (*Gets out pillbox, thrusts it weakly at* PETER.) W-water . . . !

PETER. (*Clumsying a pill out of box, grabs up one of the fuller drinks from coffeetable, on:*) Here, use this, it's mostly melted ice—!

WILLY. (*Hadn't planned on this, goes to protest.*) N-no, you better not give— (*But* PETER *is forcing pill between his lips, following with ill-held drink, most of which sloshes over the neck and chest of* WILLY.) *Yaaaagh!* (*Comes bolt upright, making hideous face, manages to choke out to* PETER:) Water—more water —*real* water—!

PETER. Right away! (*Dashes through archway, exits toward kitchen.*)

VICKI. Willy, are you all right?

WILLY. (*Making distasteful mouthings.*) I thought he'd go for the water the first time and I could *fake* taking the damn pill!

VICKI. What kind of pills *were* those?

WILLY. (*With extremely "blah" expression.*) They're

fertilizer pellets for my philodendron! (*Instantly relapses into sag as* PETER *gallops in with a tall tumbler of water.*) Th-thanks, old buddy . . . (*With genuine gratitude, starts to sip water, ends up draining entire glass to kill pill-taste.*)

PETER. Well? How do you feel? I keep thinking I should *do* something—?!

WILLY. No-no, it's okay. I'll be fine, now, just fine . . . (*Makes deliberately decrepit attempt to stand.*) If— If you can just help me to the door . . .

PETER. (*Making him sit down again.*) Don't be ridiculous! You're going to stay right here. I couldn't let you leave in this condition. Here, I'll get a blanket . . . (*Moves toward his bedroom with anxious haste.*)

WILLY. (*The instant* PETER *exits.*) Perfect! Now I can stay and search without any problem.

VICKI. Say, why don't I have a spell and help you?!

WILLY. Don't be ridiculous! Here— (*Hands her ring of keys.*) You get over to my apartment and get back here not one minute later than eight o'clock, got me?!

VICKI. (*Enumerating:*) Apartment, pack, car, eight o'clock, back here. Got it! (*Takes step toward front door, stops for:*) What about your philodendron?

WILLY. (*Anything to make her go.*) It'll die, anyway, I ate its fertilizer. Now scram!

VICKI. I could pack it real carefully—

WILLY. Out! *Out!*

VICKI. (*A bit hurt and miffed.*) Well, all *right*, already! (*Starts for door, but just then* PETER *re-enters with large pink chenille bedspread, to which* WILLY *reacts, on:*)

PETER. (*Moving up to cover* WILLY, *which he will do, during:*) This was all I could find. I don't remember where Laurel keeps the blankets— (*Reacts be-*

latedly to fast-vanishing VICKI.) Miss Wickey—? Where are you going?

VICKI. (*Stymied, stops.*) Why, I have to—um—uh . . . ? I thought I'd go to a movie.

PETER. (*Tucking* WILLY *snugly in, on sofa, etc.*) But—did you forget why you came over here in the first place?

VICKI. Why I—? Oh! The *passports* and everything!

PETER. Right! Did you get them?

VICKI. Yes, they were right in the safe deposit box where Laurel said.

PETER. *Laurel* said?!

VICKI. (*Recovering fast.*) That's what *you* said Laurel said . . . ?

PETER. I don't remember that . . .

VICKI. Well, you were busy—!

PETER. (*Begins replacing travel material into case.*) Okay, never mind that. Just tell me where the tickets and passports are.

VICKI. Right here in my purse . . . (*Looks from left hand to right hand, blankly.*)

PETER. Miss Wickey—you're not *carrying* a purse . . . (*Will start carrying case off toward bedroom.*)

WILLY. (*To get her going on* his *mission:*) Uh, listen, Miss Wickey—maybe you left it at *home* . . . ? Where you keep *luggage* and stuff?

VICKI. I just remembered—I left it hanging on Bill's Honda! He has a kind of pouch-thing on the back. That's where I put it!

PETER. (*Exiting into bedroom with case.*) Now all you have to do is find out where Bill put the Honda!

VICKI. Oh, he always keeps it under his front porch.

PETER. (*Off.*) You know his address? I'll phone him!

VICKI. Don't you need his phone number?

PETER. (*Re-entering without case.*) Look, just tell me his address and I'll get his phone number from information.

VICKI. I don't know his address. But I know the house.

WILLY. (*Barely concealing his jealousy.*) You've been to his house—?!

VICKI. I drove him home once after a date.

PETER. *You* drove *him* home?

VICKI. Well, it was *my car—?!*

WILLY. Pete, we'll discuss Bill's chivalry some other time. Right now— (*Trying conspiratorial high-sign at* VICKI:) Miss Wickey has to *get going* and get things *all fixed up,* right?!

VICKI. (*Gets message, starts for front door.*) Right! Don't worry about a thing . . . *either* of you . . . !

PETER. How are you going to get there? You can't take a cab with no purse . . .

VICKI. (*Waves key ring.*) It's okay, I'll use Mister Nicholas's car! (*She exits with a cheery wave through front door, as* WILLY *groans and covers his face and* PETER *stares in bewilderment after her; then* PETER *turns to* WILLY.)

PETER. Why has she got your keys?

WILLY. (*Accusingly, as if* PETER *was shortsighted.*) I *certainly* can't drive a car in *my* condition . . . ! (*Before* PETER *can counter this, door CHIMES sound.*)

PETER. She can't be back *already?!*

WILLY. Why not? For all we know, Fatherless Bill lives in the house next door! (*Lies back in weak despair as* PETER *answers door;* LAUREL *enters, carrying portable TV by the handle.*)

LAUREL. Hi, Dad!

PETER. The television set! Where did you get it?

LAUREL. Out of the shop. The man was glad to finally get rid of it. (*Will cross to desk, place set atop it near Upstage end, screen facing toward sofa area, find the wall outlet beside near desk and plug set in, during:*) It's out of style and he said it was hurting his business. (*Unplugs vacuum, takes it off into kitchen area, on:*) Of course, our not *paying* for it wasn't exactly *helping* his business, either. So I redeemed it.

PETER. But where did you get the money?

LAUREL. (*Off.*) I—uh—I had some money you didn't know about . . .

WILLY. (*Sits up, ears perked.*) You *did—?!*

LAUREL. (*Re-enters, reacts to his presence.*) Mister Nicholas! What are you doing in our best chenille spread?

PETER. Never mind that. Willy's spending a little while with us, he doesn't feel well. But about this money—

LAUREL. If you must know, I was saving up to get you a Father's Day present. (*Pats set.*) Here it is!

PETER. But it's the middle of March!

LAUREL. If I waited till *June,* all you'd get to see is summer replacements!

WILLY. She's got a point . . .

LAUREL. (*Paraphrasing real emotions in front of* WILLY:) I had to do it, Daddy . . . because . . . I want you to know . . . no matter what ever happens . . . or *anything* . . . I—I love you very much . . . ! (*Embarrassed at own intensity, turns away from him and flicks on set.*) That's why I went out for the set . . . if you watch . . . maybe you'll understand. It was all I could think of—!

PETER. (*Overcome, quite pleased and proud, but courteous:*) Laurel, honey—I don't think you should put that on right now—with Mister Nicholas feeling sick . . .

LAUREL. I'll tune the volume down real soft. But Daddy, if you love me, *please* sit down and watch. There's a special show coming on, and I want very much for you to watch it with me . . . It's a movie, a really great movie . . . and so important to both of us . . . It's a made-for-TV special.

PETER. (*A bit bewildered, but unable to think how else to handle things, moves back to wingback chair and sits on forward edge, shrugging apologetically at*

WILLY, *all this happening during his line:*) Well . . . I guess . . . after all—*Father's Day—?!*

WILLY. (*As flickering blue light of warming-up TV starts illuminating* LAUREL, *who is manning the tuner.*) Just what *is* this terrific movie we shouldn't miss?

LAUREL. (*Since they can't see her face, her expression is one of grim and proud determination, on:*) *"Crime and Punishment"!*

(*And as TV-light becomes mingled with the sound of crackling pre-program-lock static, and* LAUREL *stands with hands on hips watching screen so she can do the fine tuning of picture, and* PETER *stares at the set in puzzled-but-happy anticipation, and* WILLY*—in a kind of fear-reaction to her line—slowly leans back till he is completely supine, and pulls the pink chenille coverlet up over his face:*)

THE CURTAIN FALLS

ACT TWO

At curtain-rise, we are in the Colton *home again, about four hours later. The tableau is much the same as we left it, except that* Laurel *is now seated on the Downstage end of the coffeetable, and* Willy *is sitting up higher and has drawn his knees up against his body, hugging them to him with both arms, and* Peter *has twisted his body comfortably sideways, so that he uses the left and rear backrests of the wingback chair for support, and lets the back of his right knee cup the right lower arm of the chair so his right lower leg hangs free over the side. The room is generally dimmer, and whenever the front door opens, the outside area will be in twilight. All are motionless, their eyes locked on the TV screen. When they speak, they will not turn toward the person addressed, but keep that mesmerized gaze. Flickering bluish light from the TV screen lights their faces, and we can hear, apparently from the TV, the final forty bars or so of Mendelssohn's "Wedding March," fairly loud for a few seconds after curtain-rise, but it will dip very low in volume the moment* Peter *speaks, and remain low to its conclusion. The eyes of none of the trio will leave the set until* Laurel *has switched it off. All are fascinated, rapt with amazement at what they see.*

Peter. You know . . . the *book* ended *differently* . . .

Willy. Raskolnikov didn't marry Petrovich . . . ?

Laurel. They were both men . . .

Peter. Petrovich was the police inspector . . .

LAUREL. And Raskolnikov was the murderer he was trying to arrest . . .

WILLY. Well . . . these made-for-TV movies always take a few liberties . . .

PETER. Interesting approach, making it into a musical . . .

LAUREL. (*Still eye-mesmerized, stands mechanically and starts slowly toward set, watching wide-eyed, on:*) Somehow, though, I never pictured Raskolnikov as Debbie Reynolds . . . (*Will hold, at set, till last trilling strains of wedding march play, then will snap set off, also snapping the spell that has bound them; as the flickering blue light vanishes,* PETER *stands and stretches stiff muscles, relaxed and happy.*)

PETER. Well, they had to get someone cute to play opposite Robert Morse.

WILLY. (*Out of trance, looks around, puzzled.*) Hey, why's it so dark in here?

LAUREL. (*Reaches to unseen lightswitch through archway.*) It's practically seven o'clock. (*Flicks switch, and room lights come up brightly.*)

WILLY. Seven o'clock—!?

PETER. No wonder I'm so hungry. No lunch and no dinner!

LAUREL. (*Moving toward kitchen.*) What about those three bowls of popcorn you ate during the movie? (*Is out of sight.*)

WILLY. (*Flipping coverlet off and standing up.*) Seven o'clock—! Do you mean to tell me we've been watching that thing for nearly four hours?!

PETER. Time really flies when you're having *fun* . . .

WILLY. Pete, where the hell is *Vicki?!* In the time she's been gone, she could have *walked* to Bill's house and back!

PETER. Maybe he doesn't live in South Pasadena.

WILLY. I've got to use your phone! (*Grabs it up, starts dialing even before:*)

PETER. Help yourself. What are you so upset about?

WILLY. What am I so—?! The *bank* robbery! Now, *don't* tell me you've even forgotten *that!?*

PETER. (*Shushing with finger to lips.*) Ssh! Don't say anything in front of Laurel. I wouldn't want *her* to be an accessory, *too!*

WILLY. How can you be so calm about it?

PETER. Because nobody interrupted the show for a special news bulletin. Plenty of time before Monday morning to find that money and get it back to the bank, as long as the robbery hasn't been detected.

WILLY. (*Is about to reply, but somebody comes onto other end of phone, so he speaks into the phone instead:*) Hello? Muriel! Is Vicki there? . . . What the hell is she *doing?* . . . *Washing* her *hair—?!* (*Drops receiver onto sofa, flings arms overhead, rolls eyes heavenward, pounds fists onto temples, then grabs up receiver again, and tries to speak calmly:*) Would you—be good enough to call her to the phone . . . ? (*Door CHIMES sound, and he jumps.*) It's the police!

PETER. (*Moving toward door.*) Why should it be the police?

WILLY. Why *shouldn't* it be?! (*Then, into phone:*) I don't *care* if it drips on the carpet! *Get* her!

(*During ensuing Scene, till* WILLY *hangs up, he will be so engrossed in conversation that he will pay no attention to goings-on in room, but will speak up loud and clear, every speech.* PETER, *meantime, opens the front door to admit* SHEILA MAHONEY, *a rather lovely businesslike woman in an attractive suit-dress, bearing a bulky brown envelope; she is about thirty-five, and looks quite nice alongside* PETER, *who is, however, too distracted by her arrival to notice things like that.*)

PETER. (*Surreptitiously shuts door, whispers anxiously:*) Miss Mahoney! You shouldn't have come here!

SHEILA. I had to. Your finalized trip plan came through this morning, and I'm going to be on vacation next week, but I knew you were hoping to leave soon, so I— (*Starts to extend envelope on line, which he interrupts:*)

PETER. But if Laurel sees you, it will ruin the whole surprise—! (LAUREL *enters, unnoticed, headed for front door.*)

SHEILA. (*Hands him envelope.*) Well, here, I'll just turn it over to you and— (*Stops, seeing* LAUREL; PETER *turns and sees her, sags.*)

LAUREL. Oh, you *got* the door . . . (*Smiles politely, awaiting introduction.*)

PETER. (*Mechanically going through the motions.*) This—uh—this is Laurel—you've heard me speak of her—

SHEILA. (*Sizing her up, looking a bit puzzled.*) How do you do . . . ?

PETER. (*As* LAUREL *looks curiously at him, breaks silence.*) And this is—Sheila Mahoney—she's—uh—

SHEILA. (*Moving helpfully into the breach.*) —a client.

LAUREL. Client? Oh, you mean at the *bank—?*

PETER. Well, I don't run a pizzeria!

SHEILA. (*To offset* LAUREL's *puzzled look at this feeble jest.*) Your father is helping me make some investments. (PETER's *mouth is moving silently; she adds helpfully:*) *Right?*

PETER. (*Jogged out of paralysis.*) Yes! Right! Absolutely!

LAUREL. (*Musing over his attitude, but accepting this, starts toward desk on:*) Oh. Then you'll probably want to use the desk. Here, let me just clear it off—

SHEILA. (*As she and* PETER *perforce tag after* LAUREL.) Really, you needn't bother . . .

LAUREL. (*Unplugging TV, carrying it off into* PETER's *bedroom.*) Honestly, it's no trouble. We were through watching, anyway . . . (*Exits into bedroom.*)

PETER. (*Conspiratorial whisper.*) *Now* what do we

do? If we discuss the trip to Rio, she'll find out you're a travel agent!

SHEILA. I know, but it would look funny if I turned around and just *left* . . .

WILLY. (*Who throughout above has been fuming, looking at watch, running fingers through hair, etc., suddenly gets* VICKI *on line and shouts:*) Miss Wickey! Do you know it's already after seven o'clock?!

PETER. (*To* SHEILA, *who has reacted to shout and looked Upstage.*) A friend of the family— Willy Nicholas.

SHEILA. (*Turning Downstage, looks vaguely thoughtful.*) Now why is that name so familiar . . . ? (*Henceforth, no one will react to any of* WILLY's *on-phone lines, which are only for the audience's ears.*)

WILLY. (*On phone.*) I *know* I said eight o'clock, but I didn't mean you couldn't come back *sooner!*

PETER. You recognized Willy's name? Maybe you met him at the bank.

SHEILA. (*With headshake as* LAUREL *re-enters from bedroom.*) No, *that* can't be it . . . I've never *been* to your bank.

LAUREL. (*With merely idle curiosity.*) Never been to the *bank—?*

WILLY. (*On phone.*) The *breeze* will dry your hair!

PETER. (*Guilt making him overreact to* LAUREL's *remark.*) I know you're wondering how it is that Mrs. Mahoney is my client when she's never even been to the bank . . . !

SHEILA. It's "Miss" Mahoney.

WILLY. (*On phone.*) You will *not* catch cold!

PETER. "*Miss* Mahoney"? I had no idea . . . (*Now he sizes her up with a little interest, even during:*)

LAUREL. And you're handling her *investments—?* (PETER *suddenly reacts, and guppy-mouths helplessly.*)

WILLY. (*On phone.*) Damn it, will you stop *chatting* with me and get *over* here—?!

SHEILA. (*Covering* PETER's *suspicious inability to*

reply.) Actually, this is my first meeting with Peter, Mrs. Colton.

LAUREL. It's "Miss" Colton.

SHEILA. Oh, really? (*To* PETER:) You know, I *thought* she looked a bit young to be your wife . . .

WILLY. (*On phone.*) Well, *hurry!* (*Hangs up, comes grumpily down toward group.*)

PETER. It's *my* fault, Miss Mahoney. I'm so used to saying "me and Laurel" to people, I sometimes forget to explain she's my daughter.

WILLY. He'd forget his *shoes* if they weren't laced *on!*

LAUREL. (*To clarify things for* SHEILA.) Daddy's a widower.

SHEILA. (*Her turn to look at* PETER *with a little interest.*) Oh . . . ?

PETER. (*Realizes* WILLY *is looking questioningly at* SHEILA.) Oh, Willy—I'd like you to meet Sheila Mahoney . . .

LAUREL. (*As* WILLY *acknowledges introduction with curious nod.*) Dad's helping her with some investments.

WILLY. But Pete— *You* don't handle investments. That's *my* job!

PETER. Uh. These aren't *bank* investments . . . I—I'm moonlighting as a broker!

WILLY. Since when?!

LAUREL. (*Whose face is suddenly joyously alight.*) *Daddy!*

PETER. What *is* it, honey?

LAUREL. Do—do people sometimes give you *money . . . ?!*

PETER. (*Caught up into confusion between her inexplicable joy and* WILLY'S *dangerous line of questioning.*) Why—sure. I mean . . . I can't *invest* people's money unless they *give* it to me . . . ?!

LAUREL. (*With joyous relief.*) Oh, Daddy, that's wonderful! (*Startles him with big hug and kiss on his *cheek.*) I'm so happy! (*Bear-hugs him, her cheek against his chest.*) So very, very happy!

WILLY. (*Baffled, to* SHEILA:) She certainly gives that impression . . . (*Then, curiously, to* PETER:) But just when did you get started into—?

PETER. (*Interrupts, because enough is enough.*) Laurel, honey! Why don't you go on back to the kitchen and see about some dinner, huh?

LAUREL. Oh, yes. Sure. I'd almost forgotten. (*Starts for archway, stops to ask* SHEILA:) You will stay, won't you?

SHEILA. (*Looking to* PETER *for direction.*) Well, I—really don't know—

PETER. (*Anything to get* LAUREL *away from* WILLY's *questions.*) Of course she will! Now, hurry, we're all starved.

LAUREL. (*Pauses at archway, face aglow with happy relief.*) And— Daddy— I just want you to know I—I'm so sorry about—about the television and all. I wouldn't have insisted if I'd known that—that— (*Suddenly self-conscious, aware that others are all staring at her with bewildered fascination, blurts:*) Maybe it's just as well it was a musical! (*Exits in a state of exhilaration.*)

SHEILA. (*At sea.*) *What* was a musical?

PETER. It's a long story—

WILLY. Almost four hours!

PETER. I didn't mean the movie!

SHEILA. What movie?

WILLY. The Father's Day Special! (LAUREL *pops into view in archway.*)

LAUREL. Listen, would you mind a cold buffet? I don't have anything I can cook in a hurry—

PETER. Oh, sure, honey, that'll be fine.

LAUREL. Okay. (*Exits again.*)

SHEILA. What was that about Father's Day—?

PETER. (*Offering her his arm.*) I'll explain on the way to the paper plates. (*As he and* SHEILA *start for archway:*) . . . Willy—?

WILLY. How can you think of food at a time like this?!

SHEILA. A time like what?

PETER. Willy hasn't been feeling too well.

SHEILA. Oh?

PETER. (*Once again leading her toward archway.*) But let me explain the other bit. See, our TV was in the shop, and Laurel thought, as a kind of Father's Day present . . . (*They are gone toward kitchen.*)

WILLY. (*Alone, stares miserably at wristwatch, then has a convulsive near-belch, which he checks, and:*) That's the last time I cater to a philodendron—! (*Door CHIMES sound; galvanized, he shouts toward kitchen, as he lurches toward front door:*) *I'll* get it—!

LAUREL, SHEILA and PETER. (*Off.*) Okay!

(WILLY *yanks front door open and* VICKI *pops in, all bright-eyed and cheery; except for the fact that she has her hair in large curlers, and carries an oversize purse, she looks like something out of a Carmen Miranda movie: bolero-length jacket with ruffled sleeves and a ruffle-edged floor-length skirt slit—and ruffled—almost all the way up the front.*)

VICKI. (*Making maraca-playing movement with her hands.*) *Arriba-arriba!*

WILLY. (*Stricken at the sight.*) Are you *crazy,* coming *here* dressed like *that?!*

VICKI. Oh, I'll take the curlers out as soon as my hair dries. (WILLY *can't even reply to this; he simply turns to the wall between closet and bedroom, slumps against it with his forehead pressed firmly on wall surface, and quietly pounds the wall beside his head hammerfashion with the bottom of his right fist, till:*) What's the matter?

WILLY. (*Straightens up, but does not face her, for:*) I'm trying not to cry.

VICKI. Is something wrong?

WILLY. (*Turns woodenly to face her, in disbelief at her density; he stares; yes, she means it, all right; he holds his hands out pleadingly at her, hoists and lowers them a few times as he struggles for words, then drops them limply to his sides, and says:*) You— are — dressed — for — South — America! Nobody — is — supposed — to — *know* — that — we — are — *going* — to — South — America!

VICKI. But they *won't* know.

WILLY. (*Hoping there's a good reason.*) Why not—?

VICKI. Because *you're* not dressed for South America! (*As the insane logic of this leaves him speechless:*) Isn't this *cute?* I borrowed it from Muriel. It's one of her show costumes.

WILLY. And—just when did you plan to *return* it?!

VICKI. (*Wide-eyed; then:*) I never thought!

WILLY. (*Stumbling grimly toward sofa area.*) I'm slowly beginning to *believe* that!

VICKI. (*Following brightly.*) Well, anyhow, it fits me better than it does her. Won't I look great wearing this in Rio?!

WILLY. (*Turns to confront her.*) *That?* Vicki—when we get to Rio I want you in a bikini—*not a mariachi band!*

PETER. (*Off.*) Willy—? Who was at the door?

WILLY. Little Bo Peep, with a Father's Day Present! (*To* VICKI, *a belated afterthought:*) You *did* find your way to Bill's Honda—?

VICKI. It was right under his porch.

WILLY. Then what *kept* you so long?!

VICKI. (*With a coy giggle.*) So was Bill!

WILLY. (*Hopelessly, knowing she can't even understand why he would be jealous of a little flirtation.*) Vicki—is it *always* going to be this way—with you and every guy you ever meet—?

VICKI. Now, Willy, I didn't do *anything* you'd be ashamed of.

WILLY. That's hardly *reassuring!*

PETER. (*Enters from kitchen.*) Ah, it *is* you, Miss Wickey!

VICKI. How'd you know it was me? Mister Nicholas said "Little Bo Peep."

WILLY. We have a secret code.

PETER. Did you get those things?

VICKI. (*Taking large envelope out of purse.*) Yes, here they are—tickets and passports. You're all set to go. (*Sets purse at end of sofa.*)

PETER. Thanks a million. Now, remember not a word to Laurel! (*Sets envelope on desk, starts for kitchen.*)

VICKI. Oh, by the way— (*As* PETER *stops expectantly:*) Happy Father's Day!

PETER. Uh-thanks. (*Exits.*)

VICKI. (*To* WILLY, *brightly.*) And we're all set, too. Everything's in the car—your luggage and mine, your overcoat in a garment bag, and you've got the passports and tickets—

WILLY. You packed my *overcoat* for *Rio?!* How did you overlook my *galoshes!?*

VICKI. They're in the trunk.

WILLY. Listen—very carefully—because I want you to understand what I am going to say to you . . . We are *not* all set. I will tell you *why* we are not all set: Because we have not found any of the missing *money! That* is why we are not all set!

VICKI. I thought you were going to search the house and find it . . . ?

WILLY. I did not have a *chance* to search the house. Let me tell you why: I spent four hours on that sofa watching a *Russian musical!* (*He is near madness, his voice a strangled scream.*)

VICKI. (*Faces Downstage away from him with folded arms and an exasperated quirk on her lips, for:*) And *I* thought *I* was crazy!

WILLY. (*Clutches her shoulders.*) Listen, it's not too late! We can search now, before they all finish eating! C'mon!

VICKI. Where do we start?

WILLY. (*A moment's indecision; then:*) Let's take the desk!

VICKI. Take it where?

WILLY. (*Who has taken a step away from her toward desk, stops.*) What do I *see* in you, *anyway?!* (*Looks back at her, looks her up and down, then nods and starts for desk again, on:*) I *remember* . . .

VICKI. (*Following him to desk.*) You know, I thought Father's Day came in June . . .

WILLY. (*Turns, places fond hand on her shoulder.*) There's hope for you yet! (*Before he can turn back to desk,* PETER *enters, looks* VICKI *up and down, nods as if satisfied, then says as he exits again, in a tone of relief, to himself, that implies he couldn't till then believe his memory:*)

PETER. . . . She *is* wearing a mariachi costume! (*And he is gone.*)

WILLY. (*Shakes his head to clear it of this interruption, then reaches for center desk drawer, on:*) Come on, before that *Mahoney* dame comes back in here!

VICKI. *Who* did you say—?

WILLY. Some gal here to see Pete about something. She kept looking at me real funny, like she thought she knew me or something. It gave me the creeps . . .

VICKI. Is—is her first name "Sheila"—?

WILLY. (*Senses doom; slowly straightens, turns to her.*) *What* do you know that *I* don't know? . . . I realize that's an incredible question, but answer it anyhow . . .

VICKI. Well—there was this Sheila Mahoney at the travel agency—

WILLY. *What* travel agency?

VICKI. (*Uncertain and uneasy at his intensity.*) Why—the one where I went to set up our trip to Rio . . .

WILLY. (*Stares, speechless; then:*) *You* arranged our *getaway* through a *travel agency—?!*

VICKI. Well, they know all the nice cheap hotels,

and sometimes they give special tourist rates, and they throw in a free sombrero you can wear to the airport, and—*mmmph!* (*As before, his hand is on her mouth again.*)

WILLY. Did . . . you . . . tell . . . her . . . my . . . right . . . *name—!?* (*Doesn't wait for her answer, but turns away from her and smacks heel of hand against his forehead.*) Why do I even *ask?* Of *course* you did! That's why she keeps *looking* at me like that! She's trying to remember where she heard of me!

VICKI. Well, as long as she doesn't *remember—*

WILLY. (*Spins about to face her, grips her shoulders fiercely.*) Not *now,* she doesn't! But the moment she sees *you* she is going to put two and two together, and everything will come back to her in a *blinding flash,* and she will open her big yap and *say* so, and *Pete* will hear her, and he will realize I did *not* take the money by accident, and then *wild horses* will not get it back from him—!

VICKI. (*Who has been crinkling her brow, absorbing all this, suddenly raises her eyebrows and announces:*) But—that's not *fair* . . .

WILLY. (*Blank.*) What's not fair?

VICKI. Well, our whole plan was that he should take all the *risk* in getting the money out of the bank, not that he should take all the *money—!*

WILLY. (*Turns from her, slumps in despair.*) The *point* is, what are we going to do *now?!*

VICKI. Why don't I go out and wait in the *car,* and then she *won't* see me?

WILLY. (*Turns to her, about to explain in high rage:*) *Because—!* (*Then stops, realizing:*) Hey. That's *right!* Why *don't* you! You actually said something intelligent!

VICKI. It was *simple!*

WILLY. (*Hustling her toward front door.*) All right, I won't argue with you. (*Door CHIMES sound; he stops dead.*) Oh no! What if it's the police?

VICKI. It's all right. We haven't got the money.

WILLY. Vicki, without the *money,* we can't even cop a *plea!* (*Door CHIMES sound again, then again.*)

VICKI. But why would they suspect we *took* the money?

WILLY. *Why?! Me* with passports and tickets to *Rio* in my pocket, and *you* dressed like *Carmen Miranda—?!*

VICKI. Oh, we can fix that *last* part—! (*Suits action to the word, doing something magical with a zipper or clasp, and is abruptly standing before us in a trim two-piece bathing suit.*) How's that?

WILLY. That's *worse!* (*Door CHIMES again, three times rapidly.*)

LAUREL. (*Off.*) Isn't anybody going to get the *door—?!*

WILLY. (*Looks Left-Right-Left, a trapped animal; then:*) Come on! (*Drags* VICKI *by wrist toward desk, where he tosses her discarded mariachi-outfit in a heap on top, then drags her toward sofa, where he grabs up coverlet, then drapes it broadly to entirely, for the moment, cover the back, sidepieces and seat of the wingback chair, into which he forcefully seats her. Then he sits on her lap, wraps overflow of coverlet over his and her legs, and reaches back of him for remaining upper corners, which he then pulls forward and clutches about his middle, shawl-fashion, so that it completely hides her head and comes down over his shoulders at the neck. The hitch is,* VICKI'S *arms are out, on the arms of the chair, and his own hidden against his chest, securing the coverlet. The effect is of a tired fat grandfather with gracefully girlish arms, in a huge shapeless robe. He is in place only one-tenth of a second before* LAUREL *emerges through archway, headed for front door, and* SHEILA, *carrying two glasses of champagne, emerges right after her, but stops before him, smiling, as the door CHIMES sound one more time. [NOTE: the wingback chair is the only kind in which this sort of "deception" looks con-*

vincing, because the "wings" hide the bulging body of the under-party as a regular armchair would not.] Even as chimes are sounding:)

LAUREL. I'm *coming!* (*Extending glass of champagne toward* WILLY.) I thought you'd like to join the celebration.

WILLY. *What* celebration?

SHEILA. I'm not quite sure—but Laurel's awfully happy about *something.* That's why she broke out the champagne.

LAUREL. (*Opens door, and there stands* CARLOS, *nattily garbed as before, but carrying a large envelope and wearing a look of intense anxiety and haste.*) Carlos—! Is it nine o'clock already?

CARLOS. (*Stepping just over threshold, door remaining open.*) I took Rosita home at seven-thirty. Her father was very grateful. (*Rubs cheek ruefully.*) Rosita was not.

LAUREL. Oh, but you didn't have to—

CARLOS. (*With urgency:*) Yes I did! Do you remember what we were talking about earlier? Well—

LAUREL. (*Stops him instantly, with finger to his lips, aware that* SHEILA *and* WILLY *are idly listening, and says, in slightly overloud voice:*) *Oh,* you mean about the *bug-spray* for our *bush?* Come outside, and show me what you mean . . . ! (*Forces him back out onto porch, shuts door to within an inch of being completely closed.*)

SHEILA. When *I* was a young girl, we had better things to discuss on a lovely spring evening . . . ! (*Notices* WILLY *still sits motionless.*) Don't you want your champagne?

WILLY. No. (*But it's too late;* VICKI'S *right hand is groping for it.*) I mean, yes. (SHEILA *keeps trying to put goblet into hand, which keeps moving in the wrong direction, till* WILLY *says:*) *Wait!* (*Hand freezes in position.*) Maybe—maybe you'd better put it into my hand. I don't reach as well as I used to . . .

SHEILA. (*Puzzled, but game.*) Okay, here you are. (*Hand clutches stem of goblet.*) How's that?

WILLY. Fine. Just fine. Thank you. It sure looks delicious . . . (*Smiles at her, but hand remains immobile.*)

SHEILA. (*Raises her own glass.*) Well—happy days! (*Takes sip, sees he is still motionless.*) Drink up.

WILLY. (*Trying to bend his head or extend his lips to glass.*) Can't you see I'm *trying* to?!

SHEILA. (*As one who coaxes a baby to take its pablum:*) *Come* on, now, *you* can do it . . . one . . . two . . . *threeee—!* (*And on final syllable,* VICKI *tries to get goblet to* WILLY'S *lips, succeeds in tossing drink into his face; he responds by viciously biting the wrist of the hand holding the glass; this hand pulls away, and the other hand comes up and slaps his face;* SHEILA, *startled by this apparent insanity, hastily takes goblet back, and will back out through archway, speaking like one humoring a maniac, on:*) Uh . . . maybe you've had enough, huh? . . . Now, you just rest there, nice and quiet . . . uh . . . See you! (*Bolts toward kitchen on final two words.*)

WILLY. (*Suddenly jumps up, clutching back of neck.*) Ouch! You didn't have to *bite* me!

VICKI. (*Jumps up, angrily, coverlet remaining on chair.*) Well, *you* bit *me—?!*

WILLY. I *had* to, before you made me eat the *glass!* (*Before she can retort:*) Now, come on, get searching, this may be our last chance! You take the closet, I'll check in the bedroom! (WILLY *scurries off into* PETER'S *bedroom;* VICKI *crosses toward Left, hesitates, then enters* LAUREL'S *bedroom; an instant later,* LAUREL *and* CARLOS—*she in the lead—rush in from porch, look anxiously toward sofa-area, see no one, then* LAUREL *clutches his hands, her face taut with fright.*)

LAUREL. Oh, Carlos, are you *sure?* On the *radio?*

CARLOS. (*Apparently continuing an explanation:*) The guard apparently gave a kind of reflex tug at the vault handle as he went by, and the door came open. They checked and found all the money cleaned out. They're dusting the place for fingerprints, right now.

LAUREL. But what will *that* prove? Anyone who handles money in the bank could have their prints in there. All the tellers have cash drawers, and—

CARLOS. Laurel, your father *isn't* a teller, anymore! He's Operation Manager!

LAUREL. And he never goes in the vault! Oh, Carlos, what'll we *do?!*

CARLOS. (*Waving envelope.*) I've done it already! My uncle Luis hasn't lost his touch, after all these years! (*Thrusts envelope into her hands.*) Two passports, forged in the names of "Mister and Mrs. John Smith." All we have to do now is paste in the pictures of you and your father.

LAUREL. (*Turns instantly to closet, opens doors.*) There's an old photo album in here, someplace . . . Carlos, help me!

CARLOS. Oh, here, let *me* do it . . . (*She obediently steps aside, still in closet, clutching envelope, and he steps in beside her to reach up toward unseen shelf; at this point,* VICKI *steps out of bedroom, frowning, looks and sees still-open front door, crosses past closet —it is deep enough that even we cannot see* CARLOS *and* LAUREL *at this moment—and steps curiously out onto porch, looking around;* CARLOS *and* LAUREL *then emerge from closet, she still holding envelope, he holding large photo album, and without looking, just by reflex,* LAUREL *pushes front door closed as they descend into living room and sit on sofa to go through album; at this point,* PETER *and* SHEILA, *slightly giddy from champagne, enter through archway, laughing together.*)

SHEILA. . . . so *she* said, "What do you mean *drink* it, I can't even *spell* it!"

PETER. (*Roars laughter at apparent punch line of hilarious joke, as* SHEILA *chuckles along with him, then he sees* LAUREL *and* CARLOS, *and grins amiably.*) Oh, hi, kids! Whatcha doing?

LAUREL. (*Cannot speak truth in front of* SHEILA, *so shrugs and makes broad gesture at album.*) Guess!

PETER. (*Craning neck to see photos rightside up.*) Hey, are those the vacation pictures you took last summer? (*To* SHEILA:) You wanta see some silly shots of *me* trying *not* to feed a bear in Yellowstone Park?

LAUREL. Dad—don't you have *investments* to make—?

PETER. What investments? Oh! Those investments! Uh—? (*Looks to* SHEILA *for help.*)

SHEILA. (*Instantly.*) We settled it all out in the kitchen. I'm putting my money in *A.T.&T.* and *Standard Oil!*

LAUREL. *I* could have suggested *those!*

PETER. (*With a friendly wink:*) But *you* wouldn't get a *broker's* fee!

LAUREL. (*Barely able to control her anguish.*) Dad—I have to *talk* to you—*alone . . . ?*

SHEILA. Uh . . . you know, perhaps I *had* better get going . . .

PETER. Aw, do you have to?

SHEILA. It *is* getting late, and I have to pack for my vacation . . . (*Glances about.*) I didn't have a purse or anything, did I— Why, what's this? (*Picks up mariachi outfit from desk.*)

PETER. Why . . . those belong to— (*Before he can say the name,* WILLY *leaps out of bedroom, scaring the hell out of everyone, on:*)

WILLY. *Little Bo Peep!*

SHEILA. (*Anxious "aside" to* PETER.) I *told* you he was behaving strangely . . . !

PETER. (*As behind him,* LAUREL *and* CARLOS *find a pair of suitable photos, take same from album, shut album, and, along with* CARLOS's *envelope, sneak to kitchen, he speaks as one who is humoring a possible maniac:*) That's right, Willy, they *do* belong to

Little Bo Peep. But, Willy, where *is* Little Bo Peep—?

SHEILA. (*Helpfully.*) ". . . under the haystack, fast asleep . . ."?

PETER. That's Little Boy Blue.

SHEILA. Oh, yeah.

PETER. (*Back to* WILLY.) Try to remember. Where is the lady who was wearing these clothes?

WILLY. (*Looks around uncertainly; then:*) Isn't she in the closet?

SHEILA. Peter—*what* young lady?

PETER. Didn't you see her when you came out with Willy's champagne?

SHEILA. I told you, I was too busy watching Willy. He was acting kind of strange.

WILLY. (*Defensively.*) In what way?

SHEILA. Well, for one thing, I've never seen a man wearing nail polish, before.

WILLY. (*Extends fingers.*) What nail polish?

PETER. (*Peering closely.*) I don't see any nail polish, Sheila . . .

SHEILA. I *couldn't* have imagined it—and the nails were longer, too . . .

PETER. Now I *know* you must have been mistaken. Willy's nails are always bitten right down to the bone!

SHEILA. I was not! I gave him the champagne, he threw it in his face, bit his wrist and slapped himself! (*As both men stare at her with obvious disbelief.*) Well, he did!

WILLY. Miss Mahoney—how much champagne did *you* have, tonight—?

SHEILA. Now, just a minute—! I don't know what you two are up to, but—

PETER. Up to? Me?

SHEILA. Well—mostly *him!*

WILLY. In what way?!

SHEILA. For one thing, what were you doing in the other room, just now? Besides waiting to jump out and say "Boo!"?

WILLY. I did not say "Boo!"

PETER. Willy—what *were* you doing in my bedroom?

WILLY. Looking for Little Bo Peep!

PETER. Why should *she* be in my bedroom?

WILLY. Why, who were you *expecting?*

SHEILA. Hold it. You mean there *is* a Little Bo Peep?

PETER. Yes, but that's not her real name.

SHEILA. I should *hope* not! What *is* her real name?

WILLY. Pete! If you love me—don't tell her! I'll explain later! (*As* PETER *stands stymied, to* SHEILA:) Weren't you just leaving—?

SHEILA. (*Folds arms.*) If you think I'm leaving *now,* you're crazy!

WILLY. (*Hopefully:*) But you just implied I *was* crazy . . . !

SHEILA. Well, *somebody's* crazy around here, and it isn't *me!* (*Door CHIMES sound.*)

PETER. Good grief, *now* what?!

WILLY. (*Clairvoyantly already knows, but offers lamely:*) Avon calling . . . ? (*CHIMES sound again,* PETER *starts for door,* WILLY *dashes to get there first, on:*) I'll get it, I'll get it—!

SHEILA. (*Somehow sensing there's a solution to the mystery, starts right after them, on:*) No, let *me* get it!

PETER. (*Grabbing* WILLY's *arm to stop him.*) Now, hold on, it's my house and I'll answer the door!

WILLY. (*Grabbing* SHEILA's *arm as she tries to get past.*) You heard Pete! It's his house!

SHEILA. You're hurting my arm!

PETER. Willy, let go of her!

WILLY. Not till she sits down and behaves herself! (*CHIMES sound again;* LAUREL *and* CARLOS *enter through archway,* CARLOS *carrying envelope, which he sets on coffeetable.*)

LAUREL. Isn't anybody going to get the door?

PETER. (*Struggling to pry* WILLY's *grasp from* SHEILA's *arm.*) Can't you see we're *trying* to?!

(*Over next three lines, as* CARLOS *stands near archway and watches trio in fascination,* LAUREL *will answer door.*)

WILLY. Pete, I'll hold her! You get the door!

SHEILA. What does it matter *who* gets the door?!

PETER. Willy, will you let loose of her—?!

LAUREL. (*Opens door, and* VICKI *enters, still in the two-piece bathing suit, but also wearing a hand-twisted "cloche hat" which nearly conceals her features, made from leafy twigs from the porch-side bush.*) Who are *you?*

VICKI. Don't you recognize me?

LAUREL. No.

VICKI. Good! (*Starts down into room.*)

PETER. (*As she passes group en route to desk.*) Willy, isn't that—?

WILLY. (*Interrupts desperately.*) Little Bo Peep!

SHEILA. If it is, she's lost more than her sheep!

VICKI. (*Donning mariachi outfit.*) I was getting chilly outside. I thought I'd better put these on.

PETER. Willy, what *are* you people *up* to!?

LAUREL. (*Closes door, starts down into room.*) Daddy, isn't that your secretary—?

PETER. It sure *looks* like her . . .

WILLY. *Pete!*

PETER. I recognized her *walk!* (*Tries to peer up under cloche.*) Can you hear me under there—?

VICKI. (*Fastening last of mariachi costume in place.*) No!

SHEILA. (*Pulls free of now unresisting* WILLY.) I'm sure I know that voice . . .

CARLOS. (*Who has been staring in manly rapture at* VICKI.) What voice?

PETER. (*Certain enough now to make the move, lifts cloche off* VICKI'S *head—now a mass of mess and dangling curlers, thanks to the cloche—on:*) Sheila, I'd like you to meet Vicki Wickey!

SHEILA. (*Dryly:*) Howdy-doody!

PETER. It's her *name!* . . . I didn't know it would sound like that till I said it.

VICKI. Sound like what?

SHEILA. Wait a minute— *I* know this lady! This is *Mrs. Nicholas!*

PETER, LAUREL and WILLY. *"Mrs. Nicholas"—!?*

SHEILA. I've been helping her plan her honeymoon trip. (*To* WILLY:) *That's* why your name sounded so familiar—!

WILLY. (*To* VICKI:) You told her you were my wife?

VICKI. Who *else* would you take on your honeymoon?

PETER. (*In happy pre-congratulatory tone:*) Willy, you old sonofagun! Do you mean that you and Vicki are—

VICKI. Not yet, but we're going to be! (*To* WILLY, *with less conviction:*) Aren't we—?

WILLY. (*Anything to get off this topic.*) Sure, kid, sure.

PETER. (*Pumping* WILLY'S *hand.*) I think that's just great! Why didn't you tell me?

WILLY. It slipped my mind.

PETER. (*To* SHEILA:) Where are they *going* on their honeymoon?

WILLY. (*Clamps hand over* SHEILA'S *mouth.*) Don't tell him! He just wants to short-sheet the bed!

PETER. (*Prying his hand loose.*) Willy, will you please stop mauling her—?!

SHEILA. (*Released, lurches for safety behind* PETER.) He'll never get married! You have to be of sound mind!

LAUREL. (*Inspired.*) This calls for a celebration!

SHEILA. What? Their wedding or my narrow escape?

LAUREL. Carlos, why don't *you* take them all out into the kitchen for some champagne—there's another bottle someplace—while *I* have a short talk with Daddy—?

SHEILA. (*As* VICKI *and* WILLY *glady follow* CARLOS *—who leaves envelope on coffeetable—out to kitchen.*)

You'd let me leave alone with the Boston Strangler—?

PETER. I'll be right there.

SHEILA. (*Exiting apprehensively toward kitchen.*) Well, if I scream, come running! The only reason I'm going at all is I need that drink very badly! (*Vanishes through archway.*)

LAUREL. Daddy—Miss Mahoney *isn't* a client, is she!

PETER. (*Nonplussed, but tired of deception.*) Well . . .

LAUREL. And you've never been a broker in your life, have you!

PETER. (*After a few half-completed shrugs and fidgets:*) Um . . . Not so's you'd notice it, no.

LAUREL. (*With combined pleasure and sadness at his honesty.*) I knew it! I knew there was something odd going on!

PETER. How did you figure it out?

LAUREL. For one thing—it seemed odd that she'd know Miss Wickey—even if she knew her by the wrong name—and that she'd be planning her honeymoon for her . . .

PETER. Yes, I guess that *did* kind of bollix up our cover story . . .

LAUREL. What were you covering up? Who *is* Miss Mahoney?

PETER. I guess I may as well confess—she's a travel agent.

LAUREL. (*Her worst fears confirmed, turns away weepily.*) Oh, Daddy—!

PETER. (*Bewildered by her intensity.*) Honey, there's nothing wrong with being a travel agent . . . ?!

LAUREL. But exactly *where* were you planning to *travel?!* (*Faces him somberly.*) As if I hadn't already guessed!

PETER. (*More stymied than guilty, now.*) So you guessed! Okay. But I don't see why you're upset . . . ?!

LAUREL. Oh, Daddy, have you lost *all* sense of decency?

PETER. (*Truly at sea.*) Honey, wait, there seems to be some confusion here. Yes, I lied about Miss Mahoney, but I thought I had a good motive. See, I *had* to keep you in the dark—

LAUREL. It's not lying about Miss Mahoney, Daddy. It's the *rest* of the deception! I—I don't know how to tell you . . . ! (PETER *takes her hand gently, if uncertainly; this seems to calm her down a bit, as he asks sincerely:*)

PETER. Okay, now, honey, what is it you want to tell me? I know there's something important on your mind.

LAUREL. Daddy . . . you'd better sit down . . .

PETER. (*Puzzled, turns swivel chair so it faces away from desk, sits there attentively looking up at her.*) All set, sweetheart. What is it?

LAUREL. (*Cannot look him in face for this; averts her eyes.*) Daddy—today, just after you came home from work . . . I accidentally opened your attache case . . .

PETER. (*With a half-glance toward his bedroom which she doesn't see, puzzled at first, then comprehending as he turns back.*) . . . Oh! . . .

LAUREL. (*Now able to face him.*) I didn't mean to look—but it just spilled out on the floor—

PETER. Sure, honey, I understand. And you put two-and-two together . . .

LAUREL. (*Miserably.*) It wasn't hard to figure out what you were up to . . .

PETER. (*Stands.*) I guess I should never try to surprise you, you're too smart.

LAUREL. *Surprise* me?! Daddy, I almost went into *shock!*

PETER. I—I thought it would be nice to get *away* . . .

LAUREL. Oh, Daddy, you don't think I'd *tell—?!* You can *still* get away!

PETER. *I* can? I was planning on *you* coming *with* me . . .

LAUREL. Well, of *course* I'll come! I wouldn't leave you alone in a spot like that!

PETER. It *is* a terrific spot, isn't it!

LAUREL. Daddy, you almost sound *enthusiastic . . . ?!*

PETER. Not enthusiastic, *excited!* Aren't *you* excited?

LAUREL. You should have *come* to me, *first*. Talked it over . . .

PETER. You know, that's just what Miss Wickey said.

LAUREL. *She* knows about it?

PETER. She helped me set the whole thing up.

LAUREL. *Miss Wickey?!*

PETER. Well, there were quite a few details to iron out. But she planned the whole thing.

LAUREL. *Miss Wickey?!*

PETER. She may be kind of silly about some things, but in matters like this she's got quite a head on her shoulders—her shoulders aren't bad, either.

LAUREL. *Miss Wickey?!*

PETER. Laurel, honey, why do you keep saying *"Miss Wickey"* like that?

VICKI. (*Pops in through archway.*) Did somebody call me?

PETER. Oh. No, but you may as well come in, anyway, Miss Wickey. Laurel found out everything. (*To* LAUREL:) Didn't you, honey!

LAUREL. (*Absolutely dazed.*) Excuse me, I think I need some of that champagne . . . (*Exits to kitchen.*)

VICKI. Found out everything about what?

PETER. The trip to Rio. She spotted the travel pamphlets and guessed.

VICKI. Is *that* what she said?

PETER. (*About to reply in the affirmative, stops, sensing something about her inflection, says instead:*) Why? What's *your* version?

VICKI. (*Uneasy.*) You're gonna get mad at me . . .

PETER. Nonsense.

VICKI. Yes, you will.

PETER. I will if you don't *level* with me. What do *you* know that *I* don't know—?

VICKI. Gee, that's the second time today somebody asked me that.

PETER. Well, it's been a crazy day. Now, come on, what have you done?

VICKI. (*Gives what's-the-use shrug, admits:*) I told Laurel about the trip to Rio.

PETER. (*Baffled because of prior conversation.*) You *did?!*

VICKI. See, you're angry!

PETER. I am not, I'm just confused. *She* told me she found the *pamphlets*—

VICKI. No, no, not the pamphlets, the *passports*. Don't you ever remember *anything* right?

PETER. (*Now really not sure.*) But the passports weren't in my case—

VICKI. Naturally. They were in your safe deposit box, and you asked me to get them, but you forgot to give me the key—

PETER. That sounds like me, all right—

VICKI. But Laurel had hers, so she—

PETER. Now, hold it, I could have sworn she just said—

VICKI. (*Places hand fondly on his shoulder.*) Now, Mister Colton, trust me. I know *I* told Laurel about the trip.

PETER. If you told Laurel about the *trip,* how can I *trust* you?

VICKI. You can't drag a girl off to Rio without the proper clothes. (*Gestures at herself.*) Why do you think *I'm* dressed like this—?!

PETER. (*With sudden suspicion.*) Why *are* you dressed like that?

VICKI. (*Realizes the spot she's put herself in.*) I—I'm *modeling* this! For Laurel! She couldn't make up her mind!

PETER. (*Believes her.*) Oh.

VICKI. (*Doesn't realize he believes her.*) You've *got* to *believe* me!

PETER. (*Now not so sure.*) I do . . . at least, I *did . . . ?!*

VICKI. (*Now terribly flustered.*) Please don't say "I did"! (*Clutches his arm.*) Go back to "I do"!

PETER. (*As behind them a nervous* WILLY *enters from kitchen.*) Why are you so determined to get me to say "I *do*"?

VICKI. You'll make me the happiest woman on earth!

WILLY. Oh, is that so! (*Both react, startled by his voice, and turn to him as he comes angrily down to them on:*) What *is* it with you, Vicki? Every time I leave you alone with a man—

PETER. Willy, it's not what you think—

WILLY. It's *always* what I think! (*As a curious* SHEILA, CARLOS *and* LAUREL *enter via archway.*) If it's not you, it's Fatherless Bill! The other day, she damn near made a pass at Mister *Pelsner!* (*To* VICKI:) Don't you ever turn your flame down to *"simmer"—?!*

PETER. Willy, you're doing her an injustice—

WILLY. Do you deny when I walked in she was *proposing* to you?

LAUREL. *Proposing?!*

PETER. Now-now, kitten, it's all right. I wouldn't propose to Vicki—

LAUREL. You *said* she had nice shoulders—?!

VICKI. (*With girlish delight.*) Oooh, Mister Colton!

WILLY. See what I mean?!

PETER. Damn it, she *has* got nice shoulders! What kind of reason is that to *marry* anybody?!

CARLOS. There are lots worse.

LAUREL. Carlos!

CARLOS. I wasn't going to *catalogue* them!

SHEILA. Listen, I think I'd better be going—

PETER. Oh, no you don't! Not until we get this straightened out!

SHEILA. It all seems *perfectly* clear!

PETER. *That's* what *worries* me! (*Clutches* VICKI *by shoulders.*) Will you please tell her what happened?!

VICKI. (*Now totally lost.*) When?

PETER. (*Releases her shoulders, flings arms overhead.*) *Whenever!*

VICKI. Well, Mister Colton got upset about my outfit—*mmmmph!* (WILLY *has desperately covered her mouth again.*)

WILLY. Forget the outfit!

PETER. I just wondered why she was wearing it—*mmmmph!* (WILLY's *other hand now covers* his *mouth.*)

WILLY. She was chilly in her bathing suit!

LAUREL. Mister Nicholas—

WILLY. Shut up! I'm all out of hands!

SHEILA. And don't think the rest of us aren't grateful.

WILLY. (*As* PETER *and* VICKI *pull away from him in opposite directions to free their mouths, clamps his hands miserably over his own face, on:*) Oh, God! What have I done! What have I done! (*When all stand speechless, staring at him in bewildered sympathy, he slowly uncovers his face, sighs, then turns to* PETER *and speaks with exhausted calm:*) I suppose I'd better tell you the truth—*mmmmph!* (VICKI's *hand is now firmly over* his *mouth; he sags, then gently pries her fingers away, and says:*) It's okay, baby. I appreciate it, but it's okay. (*As she reluctantly steps back, he says to* PETER:) Pete—the robbery was no accident. I did it on purpose. I meant to *keep* the money. Vicki and I were running off to Rio.

PETER. Oh, boy. Willy—what's going to become of you?

WILLY. If it had worked—nothing. I could have been in Rio, and Vicki and I would live happily—if illegally—ever after.

LAUREL. Oh—Mister Nicholas—I feel just terrible about this. It's all my fault!

PETER. *Your* fault?!

LAUREL. I *hid* the money!

VICKI. (*Not angry, just making an observation:*) Well, *that* was a lousy trick—!?

LAUREL. I *had* to! I thought *Daddy* stole it! I was trying to cover up for him. When you came over, so excited, I thought you were trying to find the *thief*, not the *money!*

PETER. (*Finally understanding, and very contrite.*) Oh, Kitten—! (*Takes her in his arms.*)

WILLY. Gee, I'm sorry, Pete. I wouldn't have upset Laurel for anything!

VICKI. Me, neither! Forgive us, Punkin . . . !

WILLY. (*Sagging in defeat.*) The point is—what happens *now* . . . *?*

PETER. (*After a pregnant pause, all around.*) Let me put it this way— I can't condone what you've done, but—I can't see my best friend going to jail—at least, not if *I'm* the one who has to *send* him there . . .

LAUREL. And I suppose I'll have to let him have the money, because he can't get away without it . . .

CARLOS. Living in Rio isn't exactly cheap . . . !

VICKI. Do you mean it? Do I understand what you're saying—?

WILLY. (*Grabs and pumps* PETER'*s hand.*) I *knew* I could count on you . . .

PETER. I've never let you down yet . . .

WILLY. . . . trust you . . .

PETER. I couldn't betray a friend!

WILLY. . . . rely on you!

PETER. That's what friends are *for* . . .

VICKI. You mean—nobody's going to *squeal?!*

WILLY. Of course not! After all, Pete's the best friend I have in the world!

(*Over next series of lines, the face of* SHEILA *will become a study in terrified anticipation, which she will try to mask; she can see the natural outcome of the cross-conversing, even if the others do not yet realize it; she will try, during their lines, as they all unconsciously converge into a kind of semi-football-huddle-grouping, to edge toward the front door, but she will be at the geometric center of this semicircle when the axe falls:)*

PETER. And if you can trust me, you can trust my daughter. *She'll* never tell!

LAUREL. And certainly, none of you have to worry about Carlos. I can vouch for him, he's as reliable as they come. Take my word for it.

WILLY. So—there's nothing to worry about! Vicki and I can count on each *other's* silence . . .

PETER. You both can count on *my* silence . . .

LAUREL. Daddy can certainly count on *my* silence . . .

CARLOS. And Laurel knows she can count on *my* silence . . .

SHEILA. (*At Center of that semicircle, now.*) Well-lll, it's getting late—!? (*All others instantly look at her, realizing she is the solitary menace to everyone's security, and she realizes, her fearful face looking wide-eyed straight out front, that they just realized this, as she remarks:*) *Hellllllp—!!!* (*And, as all others take one unified step toward her—*)

THE CURTAIN FALLS

ACT THREE

The COLTON *home, about half an hour later. [When open, front door will now show fairly dark night outside.]*

Curtain will rise in the midst of a vigorous samba, by full orchestra—a bright cheery one like "Brazil" or "Come to the Mardi Gras" or "Don't Let the Stars Get in Your Eyes" but not with a vocalized lyric. The music is coming from the TV set, which is back on the desk as before, facing sofa area. WILLY *and* VICKI, *with wild abandon, are doing a really professional samba together near the central Downstage area, having a grand time;* VICKI'S *hair is now combed and lovely, and curlers are gone.* CARLOS *is seated on the sofa, solemnly monitoring the Upstage-facing screen of the TV. After a few moments,* LAUREL *enters from her bedroom, carrying one or two pieces of luggage, which she will place against wall just above bedroom door, reacting with a frown to* WILLY *and* VICKI. *In the swivel chair before the desk, facing Downstage,* SHEILA *is seated, but hardly by choice: She is firmly bound at wrists and ankles, and has a gag in her mouth. Her distaste for proceedings is written on her face in exquisite lines of simmering fury and unease.* LAUREL *crosses determinedly toward TV, and shuts sound down to zero volume, but leaves set on, and as* WILLY *and* VICKI *come to a disappointed halt—*

LAUREL. Now, *stop* that, both of you! The only reason this is on is so we can watch for news bulletins!

PETER. (*Enters from his bedroom with suitcase and attache case, which he will set Downstage of desk, on:*) Listen, are you sure we haven't gone too far? I don't think it was necessary to truss Miss Mahoney up like this—!

WILLY. We *had* to do it! I can trust you, and you can trust Laurel, and she can trust Carlos— But who knows from a lady travel agent?!

PETER. But we can't *leave* her like this—?!

VICKI. We certainly can't let her *go—?!*

WILLY. Right! You heard what she said—she didn't want to be an accessory to a bank robbery—she wanted to go home—she would have reported us to the police—

PETER. Now, you can't be *sure* of that!

VICKI. Yes we can—if she didn't report us, that would *make* her an accessory!

PETER. She was just excited. I'm sure she's calmed down by now . . .

LAUREL. Daddy's right. At least give her a chance for second thoughts.

WILLY. Well—

PETER. (*To* SHEILA.) If I remove the gag, do you promise not to scream? (*She nods vigorously; he removes gag.*)

SHEILA. Yaaaaaaaaaaa! (PETER *hastily replaces gag.*)

PETER. (*With lunatic logic, to* WILLY:) None of this would have happened if you hadn't robbed the bank!

WILLY. Do you think I *wanted* things to turn out this way—?!

CARLOS. (*Jumps up, eyes still on screen.*) Hold it! Special News Bulletin!

(*Instantly,* LAUREL *rushes over to turn sound up again, others—except* SHEILA, *of course—cluster around her to fix their eyes immovably onto the screen. In the ensuing scene, none of their expressions will change from mesmerized, rigid attention, though the face of* SHEILA *can reflect any disenchanted reactions with the television medium she cares to show. [NOTE: Since what we will hear is pre-recorded, the onstage performers can parcel out the following roles amongst themselves for "broadcasting" at this time.] From the unseen TV screen, we hear the following voices:*)

MAN No. 1. —interrupt our regularly scheduled program for the following special news bulletin. Repeat: We interrupt our regularly scheduled program for the following special news bulletin . . .

MAN No. 2. (*After two seconds' silence.*) Good evening, ladies and gentlemen! This is Rex Rumpfeldt, your on-the-spot reporter, speaking to you from the sidewalk in front of the scene of today's daring daylight bank robbery, with some startling new developments—! . . . But first, this message:

WOMAN No. 1. Hello? Jane? This is Harriet!

WOMAN No. 2. Harriet? I thought you were on your honeymoon!

WOMAN No. 1. I am, I am! I'm phoning from the bathroom of the bridal suite!

WOMAN No. 2. Harriet, is anything the matter?

WOMAN No. 1. Yes! There are so many laxatives in this cabinet—I don't know which one to take! I'm *so* constipated, and George is outside in the bedroom getting anxious!

WOMAN No. 2. Oh, and you're worried about harsh laxatives?

WOMAN No. 1. I sure am. Tell me, Harriet—what do *doctors* do?

WOMAN No. 2. *Doctors* recommend gentle Phillips Milk of Magnesia!

WOMAN No. 1. Thanks! I'll try it!

MAN No. 3. Then, just moments later— (*SOUND: bathroom door opening.*)

WOMAN No. 1. (*With girlish trill:*) Oh, George . . . ! George . . . ! (*With spinster's abrupt surrender:*) Take me, I'm yours! (GEORGE: *nothing but enthusiastic animal grunts and bass chuckling, over:* WOMAN

No. 1 *with higher and higher giggles.*) Oh, George . . . George . . . George—! (*All sound stops; then:*)

MAN No. 2. Hi, there, ladies and gentlemen. This is Rex Rumpfeldt, once more, with my co-anchorman Fred Freemish—

FRED. Hi there, Rex. Say, you've been getting yourself a little sun! (*Laughs.*)

MAN No. 2. You haven't been doing so bad yourself, Freddy-boy! (*Laughs.*)

FRED. Next time you play golf, you ought to wear a hat! (*Both laugh; then:*)

MAN No. 2. And that's it, folks. Now we return you to our regularly scheduled program! (*SOUND: abrupt break into middle of same samba.*)

WILLY. (*Impatiently twirls volume down to zero again.*) I don't believe it! They were so busy bantering, they forgot to give the bulletin!

PETER. It was *bound* to happen someday . . . !

WILLY. I can't wait around any longer. I'm going crazy. I'm gonna take my chances they don't have a stakeout at the airport and go! Where's my money?!

PETER. Laurel, honey, you may as well give it back to him . . .

LAUREL. (*Heads for closet, where she will retrieve* WILLY's *case and bring it back to him.*) Oh, Daddy, I still don't feel right about any of this . . . !

PETER. What can I do? No matter how I feel about the money, I can't betray a friend . . . ! What would *you* do?

LAUREL. I'd talk him into putting it back.

WILLY. Never! Why should I!?

PETER. Don't you have any conscience at all?

WILLY. (*As* VICKI *listens raptly, with growing joy.*) About what? Do you know what one-hundred-seventy-six-thousand dollars in small bills means to the bank? Nothing! They're insured! All they do is announce the robbery, and they get the money back!

LAUREL. But the insurance company—

WILLY. (VICKI *listening as before.*) You think *they*

care? They've been collecting insurance premiums for years, investing the money, doubling it, tripling it! Do you think they'd insure banks against holdups if they didn't make a *profit* on it?

CARLOS. But what about the people who own stock in the insurance company?

WILLY. (VICKI *almost swooning at his brilliance.*) What do *they* care? If the stock dips, they can take a tax loss! So what should my conscience bother me about? I get the money, and nobody else gets hurt!

VICKI. Oh, Willy, darling, is that *true—?!*

WILLY. (*Shrugs.*) It *sounds* true—?!

LAUREL. (*Gives up, hands him case.*) Oh, here!

WILLY. (*Rapturously hugs case to chest.*) My money! All my beautiful money!

LAUREL. Not *quite* all— I spent forty-seven-fifty getting our TV out of hock.

VICKI. What's forty-seven-fifty when you've got almost a quarter of a million?!

PETER. You know, that bothers me—I could have *sworn* the bank had better cash assets than *that* in the vault . . . !

WILLY. It must be all. I emptied every shelf, every bin. Maybe the rest of it is all out being invested—?

VICKI. Oh, we can talk about that on the plane! Come on, it's nearly eight-fifteen!

LAUREL. Daddy, do we *have* to escape *with* them?

PETER. Honey, I don't know what else to do—if we stay here, and the police ask questions, we'll wind up in jail. I'd much rather wind up in Rio . . .

LAUREL. Well . . .

CARLOS. Mister Colton—just one thing—what about . . . *her?* (*Indicates* SHEILA, *who grows uneasily alert.*)

VICKI. Yeah. I mean, we can't all just leave her tied to a chair.

WILLY. Oh, she can slip out of those knots in an hour.

LAUREL. But what if she can't?

WILLY. We could leave her a dull knife, to cut her way slowly free.

PETER. She might drop it.

WILLY. Okay, we free *one* arm, and leave her a plateful of food on the desk.

CARLOS. And when *that's* gone?

WILLY. Well—we could take her out of the chair, put her down on the floor, and she could crawl on her belly to the phone— (SHEILA *starts making* mmmmmph-*noises.*)

PETER. (*Goes to her, places hand fondly on shoulder.*) I know, I know. And I only wish—I wish we had met under different circumstances . . . (*Almost chattily:*) You know, basically I'm a pretty decent person! (*She* mmmphs *again.*) I knew you'd say that.

LAUREL. Daddy, I can't! It's no use, and I'm sorry, but I just can't! We've got to stay. *Let* Willy and Vicki go. But somebody has to be here to release Miss Mahoney—!

VICKI. Willy, don't argue. She said we could go. Come on, or we'll miss that plane!

CARLOS. (*Points at screen.*) Hold it! There's another news bulletin! (*As group clusters about him, he turns up volume, and:*)

MAN NO. 2. Rex Rumpfeldt here, ladies and gentlemen! The state police are blocking all highways, and have all commercial aircraft under 24-hour surveillance, in the slowly intensifying search for that person or persons who today, in a daring daylight robbery—! (*Stops dead as* WILLY *turns off set.*)

WILLY. That's just great! The tickets, the passports, the money—and no plane!

VICKI. Oh, Willy, what are we going to do?!

CARLOS. Wait a minute! My uncle Quinto—he's a pilot—has his own plane—I'm sure he'd fly you to Rio if I asked him—!

LAUREL. Carlos, you're helping the bank robbers escape?!

CARLOS. I'm not doing it for them. I'm doing it for Uncle Quinto.

LAUREL. But Carlos—

CARLOS. We're a very close family.

WILLY. I'll never forget you for this, son!

CARLOS. There's only one small hitch—

PETER. Uncle Quinto lives in Barcelona?

CARLOS. No-no, not that. But—he speaks nothing but Spanish, and I know very little.

WILLY. Vicki—do you know any Spanish?

VICKI. Just one word: "Carramba!"

PETER. What does *that* mean?

VICKI. It means, like, "Oh, boy!" or "Oh, gee!" or "Yipe, what a mess!"

PETER. Don't you know *anything* else—? (SHEILA *goes* "mmmmmph"; *he looks at her.*) Miss Mahoney— Do *you* know Spanish? ("Mmmmph" *again.*) Is that a yes or a no?

LAUREL. Oh, for heaven's sake! (*Steps up and removes gag, on:*) Now don't scream, or next time this goes back for good!

SHEILA. I won't. I've learned my lesson.

VICKI. I hope it's a *Spanish* lesson—!

PETER. Go on, Miss Mahoney, you were saying—?

SHEILA. Well—I never *studied* Spanish, but I *did* see "For Whom the Bell Tolls" four times . . .

PETER. And you *remember* something!

SHEILA. It's not much—

WILLY. Any little bit would help . . .

SHEILA. Well, there's this terrific scene where Gary Cooper has Ingrid Bergman in his arms, and he wants to kiss her, and she doesn't know much about kissing, so when he tries, she says— Oh damn it.

VICKI. She does?

SHEILA. No, I just remembered what she said, and it's no help.

LAUREL. What does she say?

SHEILA. "Where do the noses go?"!

WILLY. (*Smacks himself on forehead.*) *Carramba!*

CARLOS. It's okay, it's okay, my uncle Quinto knows me, and we can use *sign* language on him.

PETER. What sign language tells a pilot to take you to Rio?

WILLY. Well, for starters, we can point to the plane —point to ourselves—

PETER. Point up in the air—

VICKI. And do the samba!

SHEILA. (*Without a shred of conviction.*) It's sure to work.

PETER. The only thing I regret is—Laurel has to go to jail *with* me, if *she* stays!

LAUREL. Daddy—you wouldn't stay behind *alone?*

VICKI. He won't be alone. He'll be guarding Miss Mahoney.

LAUREL. Daddy, I won't go without you!

PETER. Yes, yes you will. You're young. Your life's ahead of you.

LAUREL. But Daddy—!

PETER. Please, kitten—I *want* it this way . . . (*Puts her hand into that of* CARLOS.) Watch over her, son.

CARLOS. Who, me? Nobody gets me up in a plane with Uncle Quinto!

WILLY. You make a trip with your uncle sound dangerous—!

VICKI. Ooooh, let's go!

WILLY. Not *that* kind of dangerous!

PETER. Carlos, please!

CARLOS. Well—

LAUREL. We've got those passports your Uncle Luis made for me and Dad—!

CARLOS. I suppose we *could* go as "Mister and Mrs. Smith" . . . (*To* LAUREL.) Don't forget to spell it with two *T*'s.

PETER. *Two T*'s?

LAUREL. Uncle Luis has a few hangups.

PETER. Why would she have to spell it, anyhow? *Anybody* would know how to spell *"Smith"!*

WILLY. Not Uncle Luis.

PETER. I mean no one would *ask* her how to spell it!

CARLOS. But she'd have to write it on the hotel register—or I would—

PETER. *What* hotel?!

CARLOS. Where do you think we're going to stay, in a banana tree?!

PETER. You can't take my daughter to a hotel!

SHEILA. Just to Rio.

LAUREL. Carlos, Daddy is right, you can't take me to a hotel— (*As* PETER *starts to nod proudly, she adds:*) —we don't have any money! (*As* PETER *reacts to her reason:*)

WILLY. Now, hold it, don't look at *me!* I barely have enough for *us!*

SHEILA. Why don't you go back to the bank Monday and steal some more?

WILLY. If you weren't tied to that chair—

SHEILA. —you'd be petrified!

CARLOS. Look, there's only one way to handle this: Laurel, you go to Rio with them and your father— No, don't argue!—and *I'll* stay and release Miss Mahoney.

WILLY. (*Before anyone can protest.*) Good, it's all settled! Come on, Vicki, grab your things and let's get *out* of here! (*Dashes out front door with his attache case;* VICKI *looks around blankly, then reaches for other attache case near* PETER, *but:*)

PETER. No-no, not *that* one! Those are the travel pamphlets; Willy has the money case! (*All but* VICKI *react to his sudden intensity; she smiles, shrugs, moves to front door, where she turns and gives a cheery little wave, on:*)

VICKI. Well, everybody— Cha-cha-cha! (*Exits.*)

LAUREL. Daddy—what do you have in that case? (PETER *looks innocent, is about to speak, but:*) Don't hedge with me, I know you too well. What's in there?

PETER. (*Sighs, puts case on desk, opens it to reveal large packets of currency, completely filling case.*) Five hundred thousand dollars—in *large* bills.

SHEILA. No *wonder* Willy found the cupboard practically bare!

PETER. I did not *steal* this money! (*When all stare dubiously, goes on a bit abashed:*) Not exactly. I mean, it's not as though I rifled the vault . . .

LAUREL. But—then—Daddy—where did you get it?

PETER. I've had it for a couple of months, now—

LAUREL. While I've been pinching pennies to buy groceries?!

PETER. How could I *explain* it to you? You keep the budget. You'd *know* something was wrong if we didn't come out in arrears every month!

LAUREL. Well—that's true enough, I guess . . .

CARLOS. Could you explain it now that she *does* know something's wrong?

SHEILA. Yes, how did you get half a million dollars if you didn't steal it?

PETER. Well, it's like this—Laurel, you remember Len Shepardson, the former operation manager?

LAUREL. The one who quit? Yes, of course.

PETER. Well, the *reason* he quit was that he got so swamped with paperwork he couldn't stand it. He hated paperwork, filling out forms, making entries, maintaining files— It finally got to him, and he left. And, when I took over, I noticed—

SHEILA. He left half a million dollars in his desk?

PETER. Don't laugh, you're practically right. See, when an account goes inactive, the computer kicks out a card on it for the operation manager. It's his job to find out why. If it turns out the account-owner is deceased, the money is turned over to the state, assuming there are no heirs . . .

LAUREL. (*Getting a glimmering.*) But Len Shepardson hated all that paperwork—!

CARLOS. So he just kept the cards, and didn't investigate—!

SHEILA. And you found yourself with five hundred thousand dollars in defunct accounts!

PETER. Right! So many people retire to South Pasadena in their old age, an awful lot of accounts go inactive every year, when they pass on. And the computer doesn't record inactive accounts with the bank's assets, so the books balance out perfectly every year. So here was all this money, left by people who died with no heirs. No relatives, no friends, no claimants for the money. All that money, just lying there, belonging to no one. So—*I* took it.

LAUREL. But Daddy, that money didn't *belong* to you!

PETER. It sure didn't belong to the *state!*

CARLOS. But the law says—

PETER. The *state* law says! If the state can be greedy, why can't I?

SHEILA. But it's not *nice* to be greedy . . .

PETER. Why should the *state* have any more right to it than *I* do?

CARLOS. The state *says* so!

PETER. Sure! Wouldn't *you?*

CARLOS. Welllll—

PETER. And there was Laurel. I don't make a lot. I wanted to have something to leave her, someday. And the *depositors* certainly wouldn't mind. Who was I hurting?

CARLOS. (*Coming along to* PETER'S *point of view.*) They can't take it *with* them . . .

PETER. So *I* take it with *me!*

SHEILA. You know—I'll bet those deceased depositors would even *prefer* it that way—!

LAUREL. How do you figure?

SHEILA. It's like—well—your *father* would spend the money on the kind of things *they* would have spent it on—*neat* stuff, like clothes and cars and fancy dinners. The state would blow it on municipal buildings and aldermen's salaries!

PETER. Miss Mahoney! You understand!

VICKI. (*Appears in doorway, holding man's overcoat and galoshes.*) What in the world is *keeping* you people?! Willy's going crazy! (*Comes down to* PETER *on:*) He wants you to have these. He wouldn't tell me why. (*Notices money in case on desk.*) Oh, how nice! You have money, too! (*As* PETER *closes it up hastily,* VICKI *pays no more attention, but goes on brightly:*) Well, look, have you decided who's coming, or not? We've got to hurry, or—

PETER. Tell Willy we'll be there in a minute . . . (*As* VICKI *starts toward front door:*) And tell him I appreciate his waiting *this* long!

VICKI. (*Pauses for:*) He's *got* to wait, at least for *Carlos!* (*Adds, with rare logic, and a small shrug:*) I mean, he can't very well go driving up and down the streets of South Pasadena with the window open, yelling, "Unc-le *Quin*-to . . . !" (*Starts for door again, on:*) See you out in the car—!

PETER. (*As* VICKI *turns and exits.*) She's right! They can't go without Carlos to guide them! (*To* LAUREL:) Honey—darling—*I'll* have to stay . . .

LAUREL. Oh, *no*—

SHEILA. Look, I can't stand this! If I promise, scout's honor, to be all mousy-quiet and not phone anybody in authority—

LAUREL. Oh, *would* you—?!

CARLOS. For some strange reason—I believe her . . .

PETER. So do I! (*Starts undoing knots, then stops to hand attache case to* LAUREL, *as* CARLOS *grabs up envelope with forged passports from coffeetable.*) Here, honey, *you* carry this. It's going to be yours, anyhow. In fact, if we're going to Rio—there's no point in scrimping and saving, anymore— (*As* CARLOS *comes down to them.*) Why don't you take it right now, as—as a kind of advance *wedding* present?!

LAUREL. Daddy, I don't know what to *say—?!*

CARLOS. *I* do! Laurel, will you marry me?

PETER. Now, just a minute—

CARLOS. Mister Colton, you wouldn't want her to marry a *stranger—?!*

PETER. (*Relenting.*) Well—I guess—she'll need somebody to help her with her Spanish down in Rio!

LAUREL. Oh, Daddy! (*Gives him big kiss, she and* CARLOS *and case of money go running out front door, on:*) Now, Carlos, don't set *foot* in Mister Nicholas's car until Daddy comes out!

SHEILA. (*As* PETER *returns to undoing knots.*) I loved your reasoning, but aren't you forgetting that Carlos doesn't speak any Spanish?

PETER. And aren't *you* forgetting that the national language down in Rio is *Portuguese?!* Some travel agent *you* are!

SHEILA. (*Rubbing her untied wrists as he unbinds her ankles.*) Why, Peter Colton, you *do* have a heart, after all!

PETER. What made you think I didn't?

SHEILA. Now, listen! Do you know what a woman thinks of a man who lures her to his house, plies her with drinks, grabs her, ties her to a chair, ignores her screams, and in general does anything he damn pleases, whether she likes it or not—! (*Stands, her feet freed at last, on:*) Do you know what I call that, Mister Colton—?!

PETER. (*Who has simultaneously risen, facing her, guiltily.*) . . . What—?

SHEILA. Absolutely marvelous! (*Melts into his arms, and they go into a great clinch and movie-fadeout-type kiss; but then:*)

LAUREL. (*Off.*) Daddy—Daddy—! (*Comes running in with* CARLOS, *still with attache case.*) You'll never guess what's happened—! (*Sees them in clinch, stops.*) Why, *Daddy!*

CARLOS. Maybe we should have knocked?

PETER. (*Already breaking from clinch.*) Never mind that. What is it?

SHEILA. Yes, what's happened?

LAUREL. The police found out who robbed the bank!

CARLOS. It just came over the car radio!

PETER. (*Grabs* SHEILA'S *arm, fervently.*) Then we've *really* got to run, now! If they know about Willy—

SHEILA. Yes, every squad car in town will be out looking for him!

LAUREL. But Daddy, you don't *understand!*

CARLOS. It's not *Willy!*

PETER. (*By reflex, points to himself.*) You mean—?

SHEILA. (*To* LAUREL, *while protectively clutching his arm.*) Oh, Laurel, how did they find out? He took that money so carefully!

LAUREL. But—it's not Daddy, either!

PETER. Then— (*As* VICKI *and* WILLY, *with* their *attache case, dash in.*) —who the hell *did* rob the bank?!

VICKI. (*Hastening down with* WILLY *to join group.*) *Mister Pelsner!*

PETER. *What?* That's impossible! Not Mister *Pelsner . . . ?!*

SHEILA. I can't *believe* it's Mister *Pelsner!* (*Then to* PETER, *almost confidentially:*) *Who's* Mister Pelsner?

WILLY. Pete, it's true, every word! He confessed everything!

VICKI. He was planning it for months!

CARLOS. That's why he initiated the new Saturday banking hours!

LAUREL. He told all the bank employes except the *guards!* And at ten o'clock he filled a shopping bag with five million dollars and just walked right out the door!

PETER. Come to think of it—I *didn't* see any guards today—!

CARLOS. There weren't any!

VICKI. Until that cute watchman came on duty.

WILLY. That was the guard who found I'd left the vault unlocked— (*Belatedly reacts to* VICKI'S *line:*) What do you mean, "cute"?!

SHEILA. Peter! That explains why the bank had such low assets when *Willy* robbed it.

WILLY. Yeah, that dirty rat robbed the bank before *I* did!

LAUREL. I wonder why he left the money you *did* steal?

PETER. Yeah, why would he leave one-hundred-seventy-six-thousand dollars—

ALL OTHERS EXCEPT VICKI. —in small bills?!

VICKI. Maybe his shopping bag was too small?

WILLY. (*Smiles with wan gratitude.*) God bless the paper shortage!

PETER. Gee, poor Mister Pelsner. I hate to think of him tonight—

WILLY. I hate to think of him anytime!

PETER. I mean rotting in some ghastly prison cell! Like *we'll* probably end up!

CARLOS. Oh, don't worry about that.

LAUREL. He called his lawyer.

WILLY. And they let him out on five thousand dollars bail.

VICKI. Which he paid out of the money he stole.

PETER. They gave him the money back?!

SHEILA. Well, he's innocent until proven guilty—?!

PETER. This is *some state* they expect us to support!

WILLY. When last seen, Mister Pelsner—

VICKI. And his shopping bag—

WILLY. —were taking off in his private jet.

LAUREL. Heading east-by-southeast.

CARLOS. Three guesses where *that* will take him!

SHEILA. Peter, isn't there any *honest* money in Rio?

WILLY. Hey, speaking of Rio, Vicki and I have only twenty minutes to catch our plane! (*Grabs* VICKI'S *arm, about to pull her toward door.*)

VICKI. But what about the police?

WILLY. They're not watching the airports *now!*

CARLOS. They're chasing old man Pelsner!

WILLY. Come on, Vicki, let's go!

PETER. Wait! Wait a minute, all of you! I've been

thinking our situation over— (WILLY, VICKI, *and* CARLOS *and* LAUREL, *who had half-started along with them, pause and look at him.*) I don't know how to put this, exactly—I'm a rotten speechmaker—but—look, I know how you feel . . .

VICKI. Anxious.

WILLY. And impatient.

PETER. Sure! Sure you are. But please listen: Yes, it would be fun to leave the workaday world . . . get away from the nine-to-five grind . . . move on to steel guitars . . . tropic breezes . . . strolling marimba bands . . . moonrise over Sugar Loaf . . . all the exciting things you'd see in Rio—

VICKI. Like Mister Pelsner.

WILLY. Quiet! Go on, Pete. What are you trying to say?

PETER. This is an old-fashioned point of view, but—Would we be happy?

VICKI. *Would* we!

WILLY. Vicki, that's not what he means!

PETER. Sure, we could make whoopee, spend money like water—but—deep down inside, wouldn't we feel rotten about it? Would it really be as much fun *taking* Rio, when, with just a few years of hard work, we could *earn* Rio? Make it *legitimately* ours?

VICKI. But I *hate* hard work!

PETER. Okay, think of the constant anxiety! Waiting for the money to run out . . . waiting for that sudden hand on your shoulder . . . knowing you could never come home again . . . Don't you see what I'm trying to say?

WILLY. But Pete, what can I do? I've *got* the money . . . and . . . what would I be up against if I stayed *here?!*

VICKI. Not *me,* Mister Nicholas, *that's* for sure!

WILLY. Oh, stop it, Vicki, this is serious!

PETER. Well, look—for one thing: Now that old man Pelsner's gone, who's going to be the next president of the bank?

WILLY. Pete! *I* will! I've got seniority . . . the board of directors likes me . . . !

PETER. And look at *me*—I'm a surefire candidate for *your* job . . .

LAUREL. Daddy! That's four thousand dollars more a year!

SHEILA. But Peter—what about the bank loot?

PETER. There's a night-deposit box at the bank. In ten minutes, all that money could be back there. The cops will think old man Pelsner maybe had a change of heart and returned it . . .

VICKI. All except five million dollars. That's some change of heart!

PETER. Hell, what does it *matter* what they think?! *We* can take up *our* lives again with clear consciences!

LAUREL. Oh, Daddy, I'm so glad! You're doing the right thing! Giving that money back—

WILLY. Yeah, and *he* was in the *clear* with *his* method!

PETER. Well, you didn't leave any evidence, either. And look at your future—if you stay—

WILLY. Yeah, just imagine—by the end of next week, I'll be president!

SHEILA. (*Takes* PETER'S *arm affectionately.*) And you'll be a vice president!

LAUREL. And we can move to a nicer house!

VICKI. (*With no enthusiasm.*) And I can go back to taking dictation.

CARLOS. (*With even less enthusiasm.*) While I'm delivering groceries again . . .

(*Others have not really noticed the glumness of* VICKI *and* CARLOS, *however, and slowly we have two different groups Onstage:* CARLOS *and* VICKI *in mutual gloom, and* PETER, WILLY, SHEILA *and* LAUREL *in growing joy, on:*)

LAUREL. It will all be so wonderful!

WILLY. So legal!

SHEILA. So moral!

PETER. So *safe!*

WILLY. (*Clasps* PETER'S *hand.*) Pete—I'll *do* it! I'll give the money *back!*

PETER. (*Overgrips handclasp with his other hand.*) You won't regret it, buddy!

SHEILA. You'll be able to sleep nights!

WILLY. And in a much more expensive bed!

LAUREL. Isn't it just marvelous!?

VICKI. (*Flatly.*) Terrific.

CARLOS. (*Flatly.*) You can say that again.

LAUREL. This calls for a celebration! I'll go get the rest of the champagne —

PETER. Great!

SHEILA. Mm-hmmm!

WILLY. Beautiful!

VICKI. (*Flatly.*) Hip-hip—

CARLOS. (*Flatly.*) —hooray. (*For the first time,* VICKI *and* CARLOS *look at one another, and an idea begins to grow in their minds.*)

WILLY. Oh, wait a minute—we'd better get the money back to the bank, first.

PETER. Yeah, you're right. The longer we delay, the bigger the risk . . .

SHEILA. Aw, but that'll delay the party—!

CARLOS. (*He and* VICKI *have read each other's minds rightly, and he ever-so-casually turns to the others with:*) Uh—listen— (*As they look expectantly at him.*) Why don't *I* do it *for* you?

VICKI. My, what a wonderful idea!

SHEILA. Oh, Carlos—*would* you?

CARLOS. (*Carefully picking up both attache cases.*) Never did like champagne, anyhow . . .

LAUREL. Isn't he nice!

CARLOS. And it's not such a long walk to the bank . . .

VICKI. (*Overdoing it, but no one notices:*) What, walk? Oh, never! We should not *permit* such a thing! Wait—! *I* have it! I will *drive* you!

CARLOS. (*Also overdoing it.*) Oh! Would you?!

VICKI. It is the very *least* I can do!

PETER. Aw, now isn't that sweet!

VICKI. (*Brightly.*) Oh! And there is one other thing I can do! (*Goes to* WILLY.) Let me take our airplane tickets, and Carlos and I can stop at the airport on our way to the bank and cash them in.

WILLY. (*Turning over tickets from inside jacket pocket.*) Gee, I hate to put you two to all that trouble—

CARLOS. No trouble at all. And also on our way— (*Semi-waves envelope with forged passports which he has been carrying since his earlier exit with* LAUREL.) —I can return these no-longer-necessary passports to Uncle Luis. (*To* VICKI, *meaningfully.*) The pictures were not very good. They could be *anybody . . . !*

VICKI. (*With inane follow-through.*) Isn't it lucky? *I* always spell "Smith" with two T's *anyhow!*

WILLY. (*Puzzled.*) Smith with—?

CARLOS. (*Quickly.*) What time is it?

VICKI. Quarter to nine!

CARLOS. (*Grabbing* VICKI's *arm, propelling her toward front door.*) Almost my bedtime!

VICKI. (*Helping him tote attache cases, envelope.*) Yes, we'd better hurry!

CARLOS. (*At doorway.*) Well—uh—*hasta la vista!*

VICKI. (*As he drags her out door.*) I didn't know you spoke French—?! (*Shuts the door behind them.*)

LAUREL. (*Starts for kitchen.*) I'll go break out that champagne . . . (*Pauses as, outside, we hear CAR engine rev up loudly, a squeal of tires, and the sound of a car leaving fast.*) My, those two are in a hurry to return that money—?!

PETER. And cash in those airline tickets—

WILLY. Hey! Wait a minute! Those tickets weren't paid for. How can they cash them in?

SHEILA. But—it sounded like they headed for the airport, all right—

PETER. And that's another thing: The airport isn't on the way to the bank!

WILLY. The Rio flight—it leaves at nine—they could make it—?!

SHEILA. But Carlos is too *young* for Vicki—?!

WILLY. She'll age him fast. (*With sudden decision, heads for phone.*) I'm gonna stop them!

PETER. (*As* WILLY *dials.*) How? Have them paged at the airport?

LAUREL. If you do, remember it's Smith with two T's.

SHEILA. (*Sympathetically.*) Laurel, I know how terribly you must feel about Carlos—

LAUREL. (*Philosophically.*) Well—yes and no. I mean, as the Woman Scorned, I *should* be thinking thoughts of *vengeance*—but on the other hand, *Miss Wickey* is a worse fate than anything *I* could dream up!

WILLY. (*Gets his connection.*) Hello! I want a flight stopped! . . . Because there are two dangerous criminals aboard!

PETER. Willy, you're not going to turn them in—?! I know they betrayed our trust, but still—

WILLY. (*Waves him silent, continues on phone.*) The Rio flight! . . . *Rio!* R-i-o . . . *Nine o'clock,* of course! How many Rio flights do you *have?!* . . . *What?* . . . But— (*His face changes, first to shock, then almost instantly to sweetly calm, almost beatific joy, on:*) Is that a fact! I'll be darned . . . No, forget it. It's all a mistake . . . Happy landings! (*Hangs up, turns beaming to group, announces:*) To my dying day, I'll always be grateful I asked *Vicki* to take care of the airplane tickets! (*Others are about to question him, but at that moment, front door opens, and* VICKI *and* CARLOS *re-enter, with cases, envelope, etc., their manner hangdog and somewhat sheepish; they shut the door, lock eyes with the group for a silent moment; then:*)

CARLOS. Anybody want a couple of tickets to *Reno?!*

(*Beside him,* VICKI *gives a little palms-upward shrug of guilt.*)

SHEILA. I just remembered—there's only one Rio flight a week—and tonight's not the night!

PETER. A fine travel agent *you* are! And I thought *I* was absent-minded!

LAUREL. Carlos—with all that money—you could have *chartered* a plane . . .

CARLOS. It wouldn't have worked out. Vicki doesn't make ethnic jokes. (*Love returns instantly, and* LAUREL *and* CARLOS *just about leap into each other's arms, in a beautiful clinch.*)

SHEILA. (*To* PETER.) Don't you just love happy endings!?

PETER. I can't remember.

SHEILA. (*Steps toward him.*) Mister Colton . . . I'm going to give you something you'll *never* forget! (*They clinch, with more gentleness than* LAUREL *and* CARLOS, *but with no less thoroughness as they get into the swing of it.*)

WILLY. (*Is near television set, turns his back on* VICKI, *places one hand atop the set, says dramatically right out front:*) Well, Vicki . . . Where do we go from here . . . ?!

VICKI. (*Thinks it over, then comes shyly up beside him, tentatively takes hold of his upper arm and asks hopefully:*) Niagara Falls—?! (WILLY, *his dramatic mood snapped by her literal reply to his metaphorical query, rolls his eyes heavenward in exasperation, then turns to her as if abcut to chide her—but one look at her face softens his mood—and he says with heartfelt tenderness:*)

WILLY. Oh, shut up and kiss me! (*She does, with such alacrity that* WILLY *bumps the television, which comes on loudly with that* SAMBA *again, and all three couples are still happily smooching as—*)

THE CURTAIN FALLS

PROPERTY PLOT

ACT ONE

Preset:

bottle of Scotch in Upstage deep-drawer of desk, purse with money in it in closet, attache case with tropical travel folders against Downstage side of desk, vacuum cleaner for Laurel near Center Stage and plugged into outlet beside desk

Carried on by—

CARLOS:

large bag of groceries

PETER:

attache case full of money, pullover (worn on), first and second and third tumbler of ice cubes, tall glass of water, pink chenille bedspread

LAUREL:

clutchpurse, portable TV

WILLY:

ring of keys, box of pills, wristwatch (worn on and kept on throughout play)

VICKI:

long envelope with airline tickets, very bright nail polish

ACT TWO

Cleared:

all glassware from Act One

Carried on by—

SHEILA:

large envelope, two glasses of champagne

VICKI:

curlers in hair, mariachi outfit over swimsuit, large purse containing bulky envelope

CARLOS:

large envelope, photo album with two removable photos from closet

ACT THREE

Cleared:
Vicki's purse from beside end of sofa
Preset:
TV set on desk, Sheila bound and gagged on swivel chair

Carried on by—
LAUREL:
luggage, attache case from closet
PETER:
suitcase, attache case full of money
VICKI:
overcoat and galoshes

SOUND EFFECTS

Act One—door chimes, telephone bell, TV warmup-static
Act Two—Mendelssohn's "Wedding March," door chimes
Act Three—samba (with repeats), taped "TV dialogue," car engine

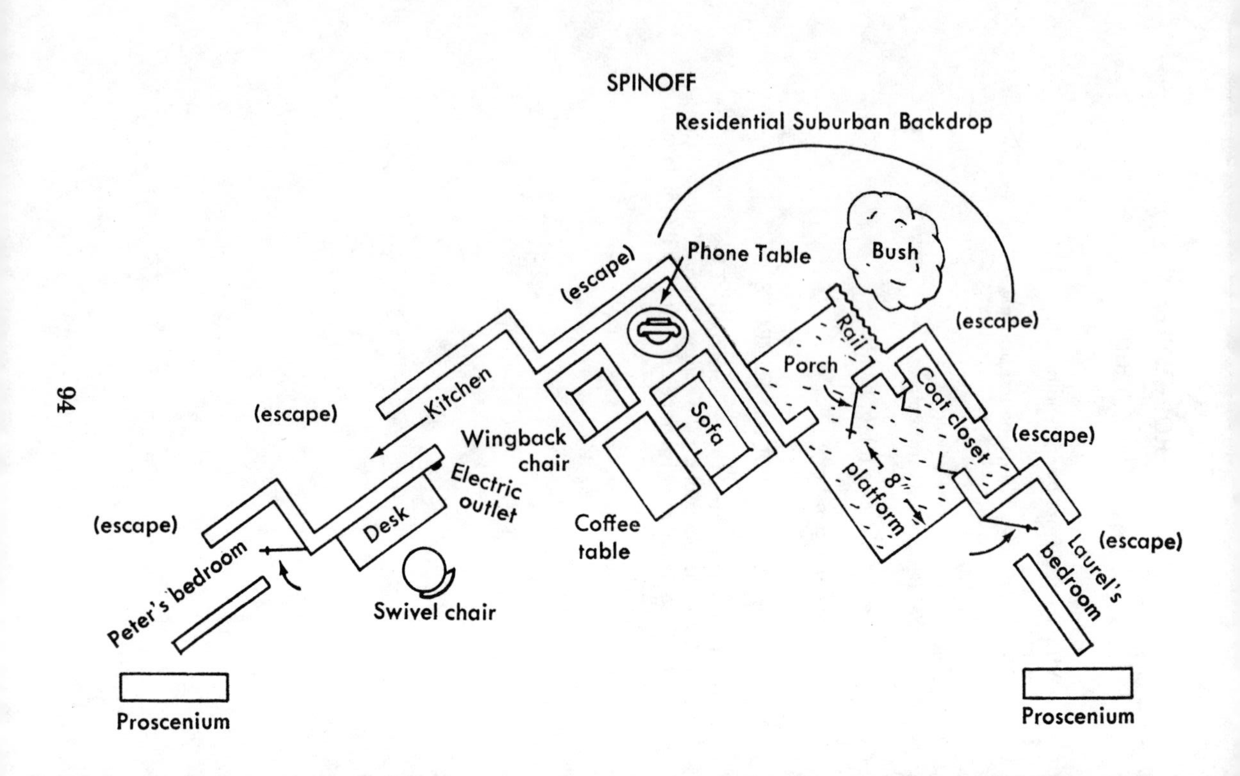
SPINOFF
Residential Suburban Backdrop
Phone Table
Bush
(escape)
Rail
Porch
Coat closet
(escape)
8" platform
(escape)
Laurel's bedroom
Proscenium
Kitchen
(escape)
Wingback chair
Electric outlet
Sofa
Coffee table
Desk
(escape)
Peter's bedroom
Swivel chair
Proscenium

A COMMUNITY OF TWO

JEROME CHODOROV

(All Groups) Comedy

4 Men, 3 Women, Interior

Winner of a Tony Award for "Wonderful Town." Co-author of "My Sister Eileen," "Junior Miss," "Anniversary Waltz." This is a charming off-beat comedy about Alix Carpenter, a fortyish divorceè of one month who has been locked out of her own apartment and is rescued by her thrice-divorced neighbor across the hall, Michael Jardeen. During the course of the two hours in which it takes to play out the events of the evening, we meet Alix's ex-husband, a stuffed shirt from Wall Street, her son, who has run away from prep school with his girl, heading for New Mexico and a commune, Michael's current girl friend, Olga, a lady anthropologist just back from Lapland, and Mr. Greenberg, a philosopher-locksmith. All take part in the hilarious doings during a blizzard that rages outside the building and effects everybody's lives. But most of all, and especially, we get to know the eccentric Michael Jardeen, and the confused and charming Alix Carpenter, who discover that love might easily happen, even on a landing, in the course of a couple of hours of high-stress living.

"Thoroughly delightful comedy."—*St. Louis-Post Dispatch*. "A joy."—*Cleveland Plain Dealer*. "Skillful fun by Jerome Chodorov."—*Toronto Globe Star*.

ROYALTY, $50–$35

ROMAN CONQUEST

JOHN PATRICK

(All Groups) Comedy

One set—3 Women, 6 Men

The romantic love story of two American girls living in the romantic city of Rome in a romantic garret at the foot of the famous Spanish steps. One of the world's richest young women takes her less fortunate girl friend to Italy to hide unknown and escape notoriety while she attempts to discover if she has any talent as an artist—free of position and prestige. Their misadventures with language and people supply a delightful evening of pure entertainment. Remember the movies "Three Coins in the Fountain" and "Love Is A Many Splendored Thing"? This new comedy is in the same vein by the same Pulitzer Prize winning playwright.

ROYALTY, $50–$35

COUNT DRACULA

TED TILLER

(All Groups) Mystery comedy

7 Men, 2 Women. Interior with Small Inset

1930 Costumes (optional)

Based on Bram Stoker's 19th Century novel, "Dracula." This is a new, witty version of the classic story of a suave vampire whose passion is sinking his teeth into the throats of beautiful young women. Mina, his latest victim, is the ward of Dr. Seward in whose provincial insane asylum the terrifying action transpires. Her fiance arrives from London, worried over her strange inertia and trance-like state. Equally concerned is Professor Van Helsing, specialist in rare maladies, who senses the supernatural at work. Added trouble comes from Sybil, Dr. Sewards demented, sherry-tippling sister and from Renfield, a schizophrenic inmate in league with the vampire. But how to trap this ghoul who can transform himself into a bat, materialize from fog, dissolve in mist? There are many surprising but uncomplicated stage effects, mysterious disappearances, secret panels, howling wolves, bats that fly over the audience, an unexpected murder, and magic tricks which include Dracula's vanishing in full view of the spectators.

Despite much gore, ". . . the play abounds with funny lines. There is nothing in it but entertainment."—*Springfield, Mass. News.*

ROYALTY, $50–$25

FRANKENSTEIN

TIM KELLY

(All Groups)

4 Men, 4 Women, Interior

Victor Frankenstein, a brilliant young scientist, returns to his chateau on the shores of Lake Geneva to escape some terrible pursuer. No one can shake free the dark secret that terrifies him. Not his mother, nor his fiancee Elizabeth, nor his best friend, Henry Clerval. Even the pleading of a gypsy girl accused of murdering Victor's younger brother falls on deaf ears, for Victor has brought into being a "Creature" made from bits and pieces of the dead! The Creature tracks Victor to his sanctuary to demand a bride to share its loneliness—one as wretched as the Creature itself. Against his better judgment, Victor agrees and soon the household is invaded by murder, despair and terror! The play opens on the wedding night of Victor and Elizabeth, the very time the Creature has sworn to kill the scientist for destroying its intended mate, and ends, weeks later, in a horrific climax of dramatic suspense! In between there is enough macabre humor to relieve the mounting tension. Perhaps the truest adaptation of Mary Shelley's classic yet. Simple to stage and a guaranteed audience pleaser.

ROYALTY, $25.00